A Walk in the Amazon

Boniface & Nkem Ossai

A Walk in the Amazon

Boniface Ossai

Paperback Edition First Published in the United Kingdom in 2016

Second Edition published in the United Kingdon in 2022 by aSys Publishing

Disclaimer

This is a work of fiction. Names, characters, businesses, places, events and incidents are either the products of the author's imagination or used in a fictitious manner. Any resemblance to actual persons, living or dead, or actual events is purely coincidental.

ISBN: 978-1-913438-65-4

This book is dedicated in loving memory of my brother Felix Ossai.

Felix will be deeply missed by the whole family.

This book wouldn't have been a success without the effort of my wife, Nkem, who worked tirelessly to ensure the success of this book, not to forget my children Ikechukwu and Ifeanyichukwu.

CHAPTER

ONE

The Interest

Professor Hendrix was in high spirit as he stood in front of the class, at the department of plant science of the University of Dartford, he just finished a lecture and was about to leave the class. Interestingly, his students needed him to tell them more about their forthcoming Amazonian trip. The professor overheard a muttering student expressing concern about the trip, he then turned around to address every concern. He then leafed through the book in his hand and brought out a piece of paper.

"Before I leave the class, I feel it'll be necessary to read out the names of students who'll be taking part in the research on plant species in the Amazon Forest," said Prof. Hendrix.

Lee Farrell, Kelvin Max, Chantell Vaughn, Christian Rock, Joel Kelly, Mallon Vincent, Terry Morgan, Tyler Stone, Kimberly Winston, Vera Justine, Samantha Owen, Beata Jones, Collins Lancaster, Jonny Galloway, and Amanda Kane." The students didn't let the professor off without their usual barrage of questions as to how their expedition in the Amazon will unfold. Lee Farrell was the first to raise his hand up for a question.

"Professor, where do we meet before we take off?" he asked.

"We'll all meet at the Terminal Three departure lounge of Heathrow Airport, by 10am on Friday 31st of May, where our chartered flight will be waiting," said Prof. Hendrix.

"Professor, are there specific items we need to come with?" asked Amanda.

"All you need to come with is stated in the list pasted on the board at the entrance of the class. Please make sure you go through the list, and if you've indicated interest and your name isn't mentioned, then you've to see me in my office immediately," said Prof. Hendrix.

Kelvin left his seat and crawled, swapping his seat for Amanda's seat, and sat beside her as he held her hand and gave it a slight squeeze, then asked why she's looking so excited. Amanda on the other hand, smiled, yet held her laughter to avoid distracting the class. She interestingly told Kelvin that the fact that Kelvin is by her side in the Amazon, means she and Kelvin will enjoy the experience of this trip together and that makes her happy. Kelvin quickly urged Amanda to manage her expectation but didn't hesitate to remind her he shares her happiness about being together on the Amazon trip.

Immediately the professor stepped out of the class, Amanda was busy adjusting her make-up before leaving the class, even as she continued her conversation with Kelvin.

"I know you wouldn't want to let me out of your sight because of the prying eyes of your friends," said Amanda.

This pair seem to have a lot of catching up to do, and moments later, Kelvin was in Amanda's place to celebrate their trip in advance.

Meanwhile Lee couldn't hold his excitement about his supposed trip to the Amazon, not only because he's beginning to relish in advance the Amazonian experience but also because it's an opportunity to extort more cash from his parents. Immediately he left the classroom Lee called his dad, General Ambrose, who's a Retired General, to inform him of the research trip to the Amazon.

"Lee, how're you?" asked Ambrose.

"I'm fine, Dad, how's Mum?" asked Lee.

His dad assured Lee his mum is fine, but quickly interrogated Lee, the smartie pants, to stop him playing a fast one on him.

He then asked his son what it was this time before reminding Lee he hardy call him except he's after the content of his pocket. "I'm off to the Amazon, dad. We'll be travelling to the Amazon Forest next week, and I need some cash for this trip," said Lee.

Unsurprisingly, Ambrose who seem to have an idea of the inner workings of his son's heart lashed out at Lee and didn't hesitate to dish out his words of caution.

"I don't want to hear this foolishness, what'll you be doing in the Amazon forest when your mates are in university?" asked Ambrose.

"No dad, it's a university project, and the university authority organised the research trip," said Lee. In a sudden twist, Lee's dad now breathes a sigh of relief and then toned down on the growling, and began a calm conversation, yet still has his reservation.

"Who's going with you?" asked Ambrose.

"A professor of plant science is leading the research team, and he's also the dean of our faculty," said Lee. "Is the school sending some guards with you? The Amazon Forest is dangerous and there are jaguars, bears, and other wild animals." said Ambrose. Lee had to be honest with his dad as he said he has no idea if they'll be accompanied by any guards yet inquired from his dad who has been to the Amazon Forest before on a military assignment about what it's like in the Amazon Forest.

"Yes, I've been to the Amazon, but it depends on what part of the Amazon you're talking about," said Ambrose.

Ambrose took his time lecturing Lee on the risks associated with a visit to the Amazon forest, he didn't do a bad of it, but Lee's exuberance seem to rubbish his dad's entire fear.

It's embarrassingly obvious to Lee's dad that his son's ears are mere cartilaginous flap that represents nothing but a fancy attachment to the body because it doesn't do enough job of making Lee listen to instructions.

"Ok dad, I'll come home before the trip," promised Lee.

A day after his conversation with his dad, Lee visits home, and this time the trip is a few days away.

His dad always make sure he leaves him with no loose ends to pull, but this time Lee decided that waiting it out is his only chance of beating his dad to it, he then waited until his dad leaves the house.

After having his pockets filled with cash, Lee was still lurking around in the house until his mum who hadn't the foggiest idea of why he's still dawdling around despite having being sorted by his dad confronted him.

"Lee, what are you still waiting for?" asked Jolene.

"Mum, aren't you happy I'm spending some more time with you?" asked Lee.

"Of course, I'm, but you should be in school, I suppose," said Jolene.

"You're right, Mum. Just few minutes from now, I'll be on my way," said Lee. Jolene likes keeping tabs on Lee; this is to keep him away from a collision course with his no nonsense dad, she then proceeded to ask Lee since his financial needs has been met by his dad what then is he still doing hanging around.

"Yes Mum, money isn't the problem," said Lee.

"Then what's it?" said Jolene.

Lee continued to pace up and down waiting for the perfect moment as he waits for his dad to leave the house, because he also finds his dad insufferable when it comes to having his way. Even at that he's also sneakingly waiting to exploit his mum's temporary lapse of judgement. Unsurprisingly, the moment his dad stepped out of the house, Lee made his move, and briskly walked into his dad's storage for military equipments. Funnily, he'd no idea his mum was keeping tabs on him, and what he perceived to be her temporary lapse of judgement was an opening created by his mum so she could see what he's up to. "What are you doing in there, Lee?" asked Jolene.

"Nothing, mum," said Lee.

While in his dad's private storage, Lee took three smoke canisters, two cans of pepper spray, and one military grade taser gun.

"What are you doing with those?" asked Jolene.

"Dad said there are wild animals in the Amazon forest," said Lee.

"And what do you think these things will do for you? Make sure you don't put yourself in any danger," Jolene retorted. She was quite suggestive in her comments even with her eyes opened as wide as a dinner plate.

"I wouldn't do such a thing," said Lee. "I don't think your professor will take you where there will be danger, and I don't think you'll need that either," Jolene chuckled. Lee sweet talked his mum into having his way, interestingly, he's used to having his way with his mum, and this time she decided to look the other way as always, and also kept this from Ambrose.

Amanda paid Kelvin a visit in the hostel room he shares with Lee. Funnily, the moment she stepped into Kelvin's room she whispered into his ear and told him she has been thinking of nothing else, but the trip.

"I know how you feel," said Kelvin.

"Yeah, I'd love to kiss you inside the plane, kiss you under those sky-rise trees in the Amazon, and even inside one of those huts that's miles away from civilization," said Amanda. Unlike Amanda, Kelvin continued to keep his expectation at a modest level, yet was keen not to dampen Amanda's expectation because she's relying on him to make her experience one that's to be enjoyed.

"Is that your bucket list?" asked Kelvin. "Bucket list, what do you mean by that?" asked Amanda. "I mean a list of things you fantasise about," said Kelvin.

Lee and Kelvin were roommates but Amanda was on a visit, and while Amanda and Kelvin were still having a conversation, Lee walked into the room as he returned from a visit to his parents.

"Guys, how're you doing?" asked Lee.

"Ohh, we're fine, but Amanda is already in the Amazon even before we get there," said Kelvin.

"You mean in her head?" asked Lee. They all burst into laughter as Amanda clings to Kelvin, as she insists on frolicking about with her boyfriend under the shades of the Amazonian umbrella trees.

"Of course, I dream it, I feel it and I think of the Amazon all the time," said Amanda.

"Your enthusiasm concerning this trip is infectious," said Kelvin. While Kelvin and Amanda continued frolicking around, Lee began unpacking his bag, he first unloaded his stuff before putting them away, and funnily, Amanda and Kelvin looked on in surprise because they were mortified at the content of the bag.

"What are these things you're bringing out from your bag?" asked Amanda, with her eyes as wide as saucers.

"Are you going after a terrorist or what!" exclaimed Kelvin.

Lee quickly related his dad's fears to them, as he hinted his school mates that his dad told him there are jaguars, bears, and other wild beasts in the Amazon.

"We all know about that but what can these pepper spray and smoke canisters do to a mad approaching jaguar?" asked Kelvin. Lee stood statue-still for while looking like man on a war mission with the wrong tools.

"At least I can use these to scare them until I find my way of escape," replied Lee. For all it's worth, Lee is a smartie-pants who likes to dare, and by all standard not the brightest but his confidence leaves those around him desperately needing his company.

The mention of jaguars and bears dampened Amanda's expectations as her disposition changed immediately, this new revelation kind of take the wind out of her sail. "You're beginning to make my expectations about this trip go sour," said Amanda.

"Don't worry, Amanda, we'll enjoy ourselves and this trip will be a memorable one," said Kelvin.

As early as 6.30am on the day of the trip, Kimberly was already in Joel's apartment within the school campus, so they could leave for the airport together. Unsurprisingly, he's out on his usual church activities, so Kimberly had to wait a while for him to return, and sadly, she isn't having it, at least not today of all days that Joel should be out and about church business. She unwittingly gave Joel a sting the moment he returned.

"Joel, where have you been?" asked Kimberly.

"I went to church, and sorry for keeping you waiting," he apologised.

"You mean you went to church, when you should be on your way to the airport?" asked Kimberly.

"I went to church to commit this whole trip to God, and as usual I do pray before travelling," said Joel. Kimberly and Joel are months away from walking down the isle to the alter, to say 'yes, I do,' to each other. Kimberly is a Christian but didn't see anything wrong with a little romance with her husband to be, and Joel on the other hand believes the opposite, and does everything to keep a romantic temptation at bay.

"I'm your fiancée, and I'm a Christian like you, but we don't have to bring God into things that require common sense," Kimberly protested. They walked to Joel's place as they continued their conversation, but Kimberly's hissy fit seems to get the best of her. She couldn't stop muttering intermittently even after accepting her fiancé's apology.

"I don't mean any offence, but I need God to go with me even in this trip, though, sorry for your troubles" said Joel.

"I've tried as much as I can, yet I don't seem to know you enough," said Kimberly. Joel didn't hesitate, as he hurtled across the room and quickly grabbed his luggage immediately they stepped into his apartment.

"I'm ready, let's get going," said Joel. Moments later, Joel and Kimberly left Joel's apartment, and headed for the airport. Even though they were a bit in a hurry to meet up with their mates, they couldn't help the fact that they were unwittingly stopped by the traffic light as cars take their turn. Kimberly couldn't wait as the green man seem to take forever before eventually popping up to give them the right of way. It was a sunny morning and her excitement for this trip meant she didn't notice the smiles of a gorgeously dressed elderly couple that just walked past them.

It didn't take long before all the students assembled at the airport for boarding, and while the students were assembled and waiting for directions, Professor Hendrix did a roll call and then addressed everyone as they gathered at the airport, before they boarded their flight.

"We've done a roll call and it's now confirmed that all those who indicated interest in this research trip are present here. As you know already, this research work will take place in the village of Humaita and will take a week. If you've any question, you can ask before we start boarding," said Prof. Hendrix. Unsurprisingly, the students are quick to cease every opportunity available to ask questions, some of which are questions already asked.

"Professor, is it a straight flight?" asked Vera.

"Of course it is, this is a chartered flight and it'll take us straight to Manicore," said Prof. Hendrix.

"Do the people of Humaita understand the English language and if they don't, how do we communicate?" asked Joel.

"We have an interpreter named Noaita from the village of Humaita; he'll meet us at Manicore and lead us to Humaita," said Prof. Hendrix.

"Do we have a guide to lead us through the forest?" asked Johnny. Sadly, most of these questions got the professor all riled up, because he has already addressed most of these questions in previous questions and answer session.

"Yes, Noaita will also be our guide," said Prof. Hendrix.

"Sorry Professor, we seem to be wearing you out with our questions, but have you met this Noaita before?" asked Tyler.

"No, I haven't met him, but I've a friend in Manicore who's bringing Noaita to us, and I've answered some of these questions in the class, why then are you repeating the same questions all over again?" Prof. Hendrix retorted.

"Sorry Professor, one last question. Are we heading straight to Humaita when we land in Manicore today?" asked Terry.

"No, it'll be very late by the time we get to Manicore, so we'll rest in a jungle lodge tonight in Manicore and continue to Humaita tomorrow," said Prof. Hendrix. Not long after putting the students' mind to rest by addressing their concerns, they began boarding their flight.

CHAPTER
TWO
The Flight

The students boarded their flight after the back and forth question and answer session with their professor, but while the flight was midway, in the air, and after the air hostess had announced passengers are free to take off their seatbelts. Amanda quickly took off her seat belt and didn't hesitate to urge Kelvin to do the same, sadly, he was hesitant, and she then attempts to pull him off his seat.

"Kev baby, let us go to the back seat," Amanda whispered.

"This place is ok, where are you taking me?" asked Kelvin.

"I'm taking you to the back seat for some romantic action where no one will see us," said Amanda. After much hesitation, Kelvin obliged and stood up as he followed Amanda.

"Ok, see you guys, Amanda is taking me away," said Kelvin, waving his friends good bye as they move to the back seat and then snuggled into each other's arms.

Kimberly watched enthusiastically as Amanda and Kelvin moved to the back seat of the plane for a one-on-one with each other. This is the kind of perfect opportunity Kimberly seeks, and Kelvin and Amanda's move now gave her the perfect excuse to lure Joel to the back seat for some tantalizing moments between them.

"Joel, let's move to the back seat," Kimberly requested.

"To do what? This place is ok," said Joel.

Kimberly interjected as she reminded Joel that her interest in this trip isn't much about her interest in plant science but she sees this as an opportunity to better her relationship with Joel away from the noise in the university environment.

"We've always been together, Kimberly. This trip is about learning more and more about plants," said Joel. Interestingly, Joel and Kimberly may be head over heels with each other but Kimberly thinks twelve months is too long a wait before she could frolic around with Joel. As far as Kimberly is concerned you can't say you have love if you don't give it, and no one gives love enough, and sadly, Kimberly's definition of love is just what Amanda and Kelvin are doing with each other right now in the back seat of this chartered plane. Kimberly can't wait to have her husband to herself, but twelve months is like forever, and to her, it's just like watching the tides.

"You're my fiancé, and you know I love being around you. Do you feel the same about me?" Kimberly retorted. She then turned her attention in anger, away from Joel, and looking through the windows of the plane.

Joel realised his refusal to go along with her love language seem to have infuriated Kimberly, yet persevered in his bid to make her see reason with him.

"Of course, I do, and we're still trying to know each other better," said Joel.

"Amanda and Kelvin have moved to the back seat, let's do the same," Kimberly proposed. While the pair were having their conversation Kimberly noticed Joel's attention was more focused on the professor than on her, and that infuriates her much more than the need to move to the back seat.

"Everyone mustn't do what Amanda and Kelvin have done, you know I love you but we just can't be copy cats," said Joel.

"I know, but it's good to be a bit spontaneous at times," said Kimberly.

"Yeah, you're right but please sit with Vera, she's alone, while I have a chat with Professor Hendrix," said Joel. Unfortunately, Joel's last comment didn't sit well with the already infuriated Kimberly because she didn't only find the comment itchy in her ears but also insulting, and could send her kicking off.

"Are you running away from me or what? If you aren't moving to the back let's remain here," said Kimberly.

"Of course not! I'm not running off, and I'll be back," Joel promised.

"Then, I'm going nowhere, and I'll be right here waiting for your return," Kimberly said sarcastically. Kimberly watched helplessly as Joel moved five rows ahead to Join the professor, she continued to fume as her disposition changed from a very lovable Kimberly to that of a scorned woman, even though Joel meant no offence.

Interestingly, the professor seems to need some company himself, and the moment Joel got to where the professor was seated. "Professor, do you mind if I sit beside you?" asked Joel.

Joel's parents are friends with Kimberly's parents' and this pair has just twelve months to walk down the aisle, to say, I do.

"Oh come on, have your seat. You want to steal some wisdom from the old man, I suppose" said Prof. Hendrix, in a jocular manner.

"It'll be a privilege to sit beside you for some hours," replied Joel. "You're here to ask me all kinds of questions, I suppose," said Prof. Hendrix.

"It's a long flight and unfortunately you're stuck with us for the next five hours, it's a privilege, and I want to make the best of it," said Joel. Moments after Joel sat beside the professor, and continued talking with him, the professor pointed at a book in Joel's hand.

"What book is that?" asked Prof. Hendrix. "Oh, that's my bible," said Joel.

"Ok, you're a Christian?" asked Prof. Hendrix. "Of course, yes," said Joel. The professor shook his head in pity for Joel, and felt the need to enlighten him further.

"Don't worry, by the time you see the wonders of nature, you'll believe science and ditch this bible," said Prof. Hendrix.

"Professor, by the time you see the work of God through nature, you'll know the big bang is nothing but God at work, and you might demand a copy of the bible," said Joel. They both laughed and funnily, the atheist professor wasn't put off by Joel's devotion to God rather he continued to engage Joel in a conversation about nature and the Amazon.

"I've seen nature at work, but you haven't. Though, you're still young, and you'll know more when the time comes" said Prof. Hendrix.

"I'll like to be a good plant scientist like you. Professor, have you previously been to the Amazon for similar research?" asked Joel.

"Of course, yes. I've been to the Amazon before, but not in the company of students," said Prof. Hendrix.

"You went alone?" Joel queried further.

"No, I went in the company of other plant scientists, about seven of us, and with three assistants," said Prof Hendrix. Joel was quite excited to hear that the professor has made previous visits to the Amazon.

"How was the experience, was the assignment a successful one?" asked Joel.

"It was quite a successful trip, though, it wasn't the village of Humaita," said Prof. Hendrix.

"What village was it then?" asked Joel.

"It was the village of Parana, just two villages away from Humaita," said Prof. Hendrix.

"Are the findings from that research available for students like us to study?" asked Joel. The professor took a liking to Joel as he finds his interest in plant science fascinating and became keenly interested in furthering his conversation with Joel.

"Yes, the materials are there on my website, and I think you'll find it very helpful." said Prof. Hendrix. "When we return to the United Kingdom, that'll be one of my assignments," promised Joel.

While the students were seated in pockets, with their circle of friends, Vera was alone and didn't seem to want any company. The guys made jokes that Kelvin has taken a bite of the first apple, and arguably won't be able to spit it out, and it's now obvious that Amanda will have the last laugh. Sadly for Kimberly, they said, Joel hasn't taken a bite of anything and has the latitude to spit whatever he wants out.

Tyler Stone had always shown an interest in Vera but the interest had never been reciprocated. Tyler interestingly, felt this could be an opportunity for bonding with Vera since there won't be any distractions now that she's alone. He therefore left his seat where he's seated in the company of friends to sit beside Vera, who was already half asleep.

"Hi Vera," said Tyler.

"Oh, Tyler, it's you. What are you doing here?" asked Vera.

"I noticed you're alone, and decided to keep you company," said Tyler. This sadly, is a bad move by Tyler because Vera is highly irritable, and funnily, she finds Tyler insufferable. She gave Tyler the treatment of a plague, as she called his bluff and muttered, telling him he has got some nerve, before asking where this illusive confidence comes from. She's quite upfront in keeping him at bay because she doesn't seem to want any company particularly one that'll engage her in a lengthy conversation, as she wants to go back to sleep. It didn't take long for Tyler to realise he's skating on a thin ice, Vera smiled and said she likes conversation, and even eats it as dinner sometimes, yet she made it clear that she isn't ready to get chatty with Tyler. Funnily, with Vera, he's about to dig himself a hole he can't climb out of without the helping hand of an unlikely circumstance.

"As you can see I'm sleeping, and I need to be left alone," said Vera.

"Why is it that you never had time to hear me out in school? Now that we're here alone, please hear me out," said Tyler.

"This is an academic trip, and not an opportunity to fall in love," Vera said, without any show of emotion.

"I used to think you liked me," Tyler said, and smiled at stern looking Vera, who remained disinterested in whatever Tyler had to say.

"What gives you the impression that I'm in love with you?" asked Vera. "The way you smile, the way you giggle, and the way you laugh when you talk with me gives me the impression that you like me," said Tyler.

"Do I really do all these things you said?" asked Vera.

Vera's disposition softened up a bit as she became more engaging, and that encouraged Tyler to continue pestering her further. "Yes, you do that. Though, I must confess, I've fallen in love with you already," said Tyler.

"Is this limerence or love?" asked Vera. Tyler tried to strengthen his position as he told Vera this isn't infatuation, this is real, but Vera had other things in mind and didn't bat an eyelid as she quickly put Tyler in his place. She told him he's just a friend, or a course mate rather, and nothing more.

Unfortunately, youthful exuberance meant these guys focused their strength cherishing these ladies bodies rather than the workings of their minds.

Tyler's smiles didn't last as his bright disposition faded the moment Vera rudely binned his love for her.

"But falling in love with you isn't a crime, I suppose. We're students and making friends is what students do," said Tyler.

"Should I describe that as youthful gyration?" asked Vera.

"Please don't do this to me, Vera, you know you're a diva and I would love to hang around you," Tyler pleads. While the conversation continued, most of the guys in the flight turned their focus on Tyler because it's general knowledge that Vera isn't into Tyler and they watched with keen interest to see how Vera will give Tyler the boot. "I know I'm a diva, and you don't need to remind me of that," said Vera.

Tyler looked around and realised that eyes were on him, and his friends expects nothing less than success with Vera, and sadly, Tyler's ego is now put to test, but trying to save his face in such awkward moment with Vera, Tyler leans towards Vera's ear.

"Please just scribble any phone number whether correct or not on a piece of paper and hand it to me to save my pride," said Tyler.

"Why should I do that?" asked Vera.

"Those guys are watching, they need to know I succeeded with you because they may mock me later," Tyler whispered.

"Oh, good to hear that, and I'll scream at you now if you don't leave," threatened Vera.

"Ok, ok, I'm leaving, but that's cruel," said Tyler.

"I hate awkward and nerve-wracking conversation like yours," said Vera. Tyler stood up and was about to leave but not without expressing his disappointment.

"I was warming up to your openness but your nagging reception has set off tremulous fear in me," said Tyler.

"Whatever, I don't care," said Vera.

"Why the animosity towards me? I came to you bearing an olive branch, but you took it off me and stamped on it," said Tyler.

After expressing his disappointments, Tyler left Vera bearing a sad face and joined his friends who are keen on the outcome of his encounter with Vera.

Tyler then returns to his seat even as he attempts to get rid of that defeated attitude from his facial disposition, most of the guys in the flight made jests of him. He however didn't mind them, as he brought his phone and began fiddling with the thing.

"Tyler, did she just turn you down?" asked Johnny. His inability to win Vera over serendipitously made Tyler the man in the middle of banter, yet Tyler tried to make light of the entire situation, but his friends seem not to toe his line.

"She just wanted to be left alone," said Tyler.

"Does it mean you can't pull down the wall surrounding her heart?" asked Terry.

"Maybe he doesn't need to pull down any wall. I think all he needs is a key that'll give him access," said Christian. "I suggest you see Kelvin for lessons," Christian advised further.

"What lessons are you talking about?" asked Tyler. "Lessons on how to win a woman's heart, I suppose," said Christian. Tyler remained silent while his friends discussed his failed escapade but along the line he decided to flow with the banter instead of being moody.

"Oh, you've got jokes," said Tyler.

"Kelvin has a key that gives him access to any woman's heart," said Lee.

"Then, I'll solicit Kelvin's services because I need those keys," said Tyler. They all burst into laughter.

"Where's Kelvin?" asked Tyler. "He's curled up in Amanda's arms at the back," said Terry.

"Please, no one should go over there to spoil their fun, Amanda won't like it," Lee pleads.

After spending about two hours with Professor Hendrix, Joel returned to Kimberly who had already fallen asleep. He sat quietly by her side and read his bible but moments later Kimberly woke up and was surprised to see Joel who's nicely seated by her side.

"When did you return to your seat?" asked Kimberly.

"You were already asleep when I got back, so I decided to allow you have a quiet nap," said Joel.

"I want to ask you a question," said Kimberly.

"You're free to ask your question, any question," said Joel.

"How old are you?" asked Kimberly. Joel sat up, as he was surprised at the direction of Kimberly's line of questioning.

"You know I'm 26 and we are both doing our master's degree, but why're you asking?" Joel asked curiously.

"What about the professor, how old is he?" Kimberly prodded him further.

"Why would the professor's age be my problem? But he would be between 60 years and 65 years, I suppose," said Joel.

"You're a young man in his prime, stop attaching yourself to an old man, except you're an old man residing in the body of a youth," said Kimberly.

"Oh my God, Kimberly. Why're you sounding like this!" Joel exclaimed. Kimberly wasn't letting Joel off easily as she continued to badger him into being her kind of man.

"Stop being too predictable and try to be spontaneous at times," said Kimberly.

"Am I that easy to predict?" asked Joel. "When you associate yourself with your mates all this nostalgia will go away and you'll begin to think like a young man," said Kimberly.

"But now that I've associated myself with the professor....," said Joel. Kimberly interjected.

"You'll think like an old professor and unfortunately my dear, you'll suddenly become boring," said Kimberly. Unfortunately, Kimberly has suddenly become more than a handful, a piece of work sort of, and Joel knew this drama with Kimberly will continue unabated unless he does something about it. Instead of sitting right by her side and looking like the ghost of Christmas past, Joel decided to wriggle himself out of Kimberly's wrath.

"Ok, come here; let me compensate you with a big hug," said Joel. "Hmm, now you're trying to act outside the box," said Kimberly, with a smile.

"You mean, spontaneous?" asked Joel.

"Yeah," said Kimberly. Joel laughed to lighten the atmosphere, she suddenly joined him in the laughter, and interestingly, the tense ambience became friendly.

"It's pretty funny, isn't it? That after all this while you're now realising I'm not spontaneous," said Joel.

"You won't see what you don't want to see about yourself," Kimberly retorted.

After a long haul flight, Professor Hendrix and the students arrived at the local Manicore Airport, where his friend, Professor Santos Da Silva from the University of Therry in Brazil, was already waiting.

"Hello Professor, how was your flight?" asked Prof. Santos.

"Our flight was perfect, and good to see you," said Prof. Hendrix.

After the handshakes, Professor Hendrix turned to his students and said, "Meet my friend, Professor Santos Da Silva from the University of Therry, Brazil," he said. Then the students unwittingly chorused.

"Hello Professor." In the usual manner Professor Santos responded.

"Hello students, welcome to the Amazon," he said. After spending some few minutes exchanging pleasantries, the students remained quiet as they listen to what their professor had to say.

"Are you prepared for us? What about our guide from the village of Humaita?" asked Prof. Hendrix.

"Here he is," Prof. Santos said, as he points to Noaita, who's standing by one of the buses. Professor Hendrix then shifted his focus to Noaita.

"Hello, how're you?" asked Prof. Hendrix.

"I'm fine, Professor, and you're welcome to our jungle," said Noaita, as he stretched his hand for a handshake with the professor. Professor Hendrix's concern is the ability of their tour guide to hear and speak the English language fluently, and funny enough Noaita greeted them fluently in English. Meaning, that concern has been resolved.

"Good to know you understand English," said Prof. Hendrix. Funnily, Professor Santos interjected, and reminded his friend that he should know that he would give him the right person to be their guide. The students are itching to get going as they are already showing signs of fatigue from a long haul trip and needed to give their feet a rest.

"Can we start going to the lodge? It was quite a long trip," said Prof. Hendrix.

"Yes, let's go. The buses are ready," said Prof. Santos. The students boarded the two buses provided and were transported to the jungle lodge, where they were meant to pass the night.

"Professor, I reserved seven rooms for you and your students," said Prof. Santos. "Ok, that's good. What about you?" asked Prof. Hendrix. "I've reserved a room for myself and another for Noaita," Prof. Santos.

Moments later, the buses arrived at the jungle lodge where the students were meant to rest for the night, and they all alighted and made their way to the reception. Professor Hendrix gathered the students together.

"Students, we have seven rooms reserved for us. I'll have one of them to myself, and the rest will be shared, three rooms each for the boys, and the other three for the ladies," said Prof. Hendrix.

While some of the guys were busying themselves trying to chat the ladies up, some others are tired of dawdling around.

"Guys, let's go to our rooms," said Terry. Terry's call made the guys to start making their way to their rooms but Kelvin was the last to heed Terry's call. This is because the moment Kelvin turned to join the others, Amanda pulled him aside.

"Let's get a separate room for ourselves," said Amanda. Kelvin quickly reminded Amanda that their course mates won't allow him and Amanda alone to have one of the six rooms to themselves. Amanda on the other hand replied to Kevin, saying that wasn't what she meant.

"Then what do you mean?" asked Kelvin. Amanda used her seductive skills to persuade Kelvin into agreeing to get a separate room.

"Baby, let's pay for a room, by ourselves," Amanda whispered.

"Ok, if that's all that's needed to make my queen happy, then I'll do just that," said Kelvin. Other ladies in her company watched as Amanda went her separate way with Kelvin.

"Where are you going, Amanda? asked Samantha. "Kelvin and I are paying for a room, so we don't inconvenience you girls," said Amanda. Unsurprisingly, keen-eyed watchers looked on as Amanda walked away holding hands with Kelvin.

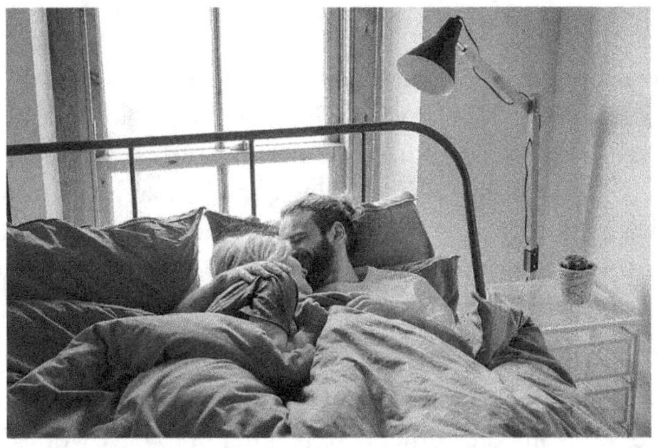

Sadly, Amanda's move unwittingly provoked an immediate reaction from Kimberly, who then pursued Joel and when she got to him, she began flattering him with hugs.

"Babe, let's get a room for ourselves," said Kimberly.

"That won't be possible, because ladies are to stay in different rooms from the guys," said Joel.

"I mean we should pay for a room for ourselves," said Kimberly. Joel seems determine to join the guys but Kimberly doesn't seem to be letting him off the hook, as she insisted they have the cash to get a separate room for themselves.

"Why? There are rooms already provided," said Joel.

"But Amanda and Kelvin are paying for a room for themselves, what's stopping us? Kimberly protested.

"Babe, I don't think it's appropriate, we mustn't do everything Kelvin and Amanda do," said Joel.

This is a university course work and has nothing to do with Amanda's 50 shades of grey, but Joel's perception of Amanda's interest in this trip being all about 50 shades of grey and nothing else, is one more of Joel's mistake that adds to the litany of mistakes and excuses that got Kimberly asking herself if she's asking for too much.

Unfortunately for Joel there's nothing Kimberley desires more than a university course work with some touch of 50 shades of grey. She looked at Joel with this intensity and asked if that is too much to ask and why isn't he willing to make that happen for her. Being caught up in mass hysteria isn't his thing, and obviously the fate of this relationship is now tittering on the edge. She made it clear in no uncertain terms to Joel that this trip will be awfully boring if the giggles and the frolicking are left out.

Effort to prevail on Kimberley to stop stringing him along in the name of knowing each other better seem not to have worked, and her constant push for some romantic touch in their relationship seem to be getting under Joel's skin even as he tried making light of her constant bickering. He then made it clear to Kimberley that her attempts to tie him to her apron in the name of romance will be nothing short of double jeopardy for him because she already has him.

Sadly, Kimberly thought that a simple but profound gesture such as this will help her and her fiancée bond better, but he isn't budging. In an outburst of anger, Kimberly turned her back to her unyielding fiancé and kissed her teeth.

The lifestyle Kimberly expects of her fiancée is in sharp contrast with Joel's whom she sometimes finds tiresome because she considers him rustic, crude and a church guy who does nothing but spent most of his time on outdated library books. As far as she's concerned the likes of Joel is a cautionary tale of youthfulness. Serendipitously, Joel's sanguine nature makes her his captive audience, just that she doesn't' like the idea of leaving the romance until after marriage.

"Why can't you just blow my heart with surprises?" she asked, then left Joel angrily and joined the other girls. Kimberly stopped again suddenly and returned to Joel, she then dragged Joel further away to the side for a serious telling off. She threatened to tell her dad that her relationship with Joel isn't working out, saying people go the extra mile just to make their fiancée happy, and accused Joel of not lifting even a finger to make her happy.

Their relationship is the product of two conservative Christian parents who feel their children are suited for each other in marriage. Now that cracks are beginning to emerge as a consequence of their level of maturity in the faith, reverting to their parents is now Kimberley's next option.

Amanda seems to be hearing noise like the sound of music from a distance, she immediately got up from bed and inched closer to the window, and then slides the curtain a bit to see what the noise was about. She couldn't believe her eyes when she realised there is a festival celebration going on out there. She turned around and screamed out to her boyfriend. "Kev, see, see, this is interesting!" Exclaimed Amanda.

Kelvin jumped out of the bed and rushed to the window to see what Amanda was about. "Oh my God, Amanda. This is beautiful," replied Kelvin.

She and Kelvin rushed out of their room in excitement and alerted other students of the happenings just a stone throw away from their lodge.

The students rushed outside in excitement to see what it was Kelvin and Amanda was about, funnily they loved what they saw and hurtled towards the crowd. Tyler looked around and couldn't find Vera among the girls, he immediately stopped and asked Beata of Vera's whereabouts. "She's cooped up in the room," said Beata.

"Why, she can't be all by herself in there,' replied Tyler.

"I don't know about that, but I think she isn't particularly disposed to crowd," Beata retorted.

Tyler realised his questions has suddenly become one too many for Beata who is keen to join the others, and his questions are holding her back. He immediately allowed her to continue while he ran back to the jungle lodge to seek out Vera.

Somehow, he stumbled into Professor Hendrix who came out of his room for a word with the bar staff. He immediately asked Tyler where he's coming from, Tyler replied the professor that there is a festival going on just by the corner, with lots of music and traditional art displays. "I heard the noise that sounds like crowd of people from a distance but can't make out what it's about. But why did you guys step out of the lodge without first informing me?" Asked Prof. Hendrix.

"That's what I just came to do," replied Tyler.

Tyler's ingenious response saved the day for his colleagues, yet the professor cautioned that they should be careful and shouldn't stray too far.

Tyler told the professor that the festival seems interesting and urged him to join them, saying it will help take away the stress of the long flight. Professor Hendrix seem not interested and told Tyler he's fine staying back in the lodge.

After managing the situation with the professor, Tyler then rushed to get Vera.

He knocked the door and called out Vera's name, she didn't answer at first but after calling her name a second time she asked him what it is he wants from her. Vera thinks Tyler want to take the opportunity of her being alone in the room to crawl into her life.

"I realised you aren't with the girls, so I came back to get you," replied Tyler.

"Stop bothering me, I am not interested," said Vera.

The festival seems nice and all the girls are enjoying it, I want you to come along," he insisted.

"I am not interested, go away, Tyler," she retorted.

Tyler stuttered a bit, it was as if he should disappear inside himself after being harshly rejected by Vera. He then turned around and left feeling quite disappointed after the brutal treatment by Vera. It's like telling the pig, enough of your grunts.

Someone from the crowd inched close to one of the students. He's John Griffiths a British citizen now based in Brazil and married to one of the natives of Manicore. He came with his wife from Sao Paulo for the festival and they are now planning their return to Sao Paulo as the one-week festival ends today, they will be returning to Sao Paulo tomorrow.

While Amanda and Kelvin were yet speaking, John introduces himself, saying he knew they are British Nationals, from their accents.

"I'm Amanda, and this Kelvin, my boyfriend. You're English, do you live here? I mean, Manicore," asked Amanda. "Of course not, but I am married to a native. That's my wife over there," replied John.

After his conversation with Amanda and Kelvin, John was introduced to other students who came out to enjoy the festival.

"You mean you came all the way from the UK for this festival?" Amanda probed further.

John immediately called his wife, Jain, to come over, she came immediately and said hello and the brief introduction that followed. She then hurriedly returned to her folks leaving John to continue his conversation with his British friends.

John had to take his time to explain to these curious students that he's resident in Sao Paulo, Brazil, that he came with his wife days ago for this much talked about festival. This festival is celebrated by people who come from far and near the length and breadth of Brazil. Some of the students joined in the dancing as they prefer not to spectate alone.

In a throw of passion, Amanda passed her hand around Kelvin's shoulder "I told you, Kev, this adventure will blow your mind, thrill your emotions and wow your eyes!" Exclaimed Amanda, with smiles wreathed all over her face.

As far as Amanda is concerned this isn't the usual academic research trip, she considers this a social expedition where housekeeping rules matters less. Kelvin continued smiling as he tags along with Amanda who obviously has too much to look forward to.

Amanda has been awfully good at making sure her bucket list of activities lined up for this adventure plus the extras that came along the way aren't missed. It's now obvious to Kelvin that Amanda's fantasy concerning this trip knows no bound.

The next morning, the students got ready quite early and hopped on their busses, and then drove into the village of Humaita, the ground zero of their science research, and then all the students alighted.

"My visitors, you're welcome to my village," said Noaita.

"Please Noaita, you need to show them to their huts and tell them everything they need to know," said Prof. Santos.

"Ok, I've reserved these seven huts for you. The professor will have one and the students will share the other six," said Noaita. The students were all looking like people on a different planet as they stood in the mist of the Amazonian people. Their excitement isn't because they look different from the natives but the fact that text book stories are now becoming a real life experience. Interestingly, Johnny has something else in mind.

"Professor, why're they always reserving seven rooms for us?" Johnny asked curiously. "That was what I requested," said Prof. Hendrix.

"I was just surprised at that number seven surfacing with each reservation that was made," said Johnny. After showing them to their huts, some of the students are itching to walk around the village to at least get a glimpse of what the forest will look like.

"Please my visitors, from tomorrow when you start your research, I'll be with you each time you enter the forest," said Noaita.

Professor Hendrix then asked the students to go into their huts, reminding them the guys have three huts, and ladies the other three.

"You can all relax in your huts until tomorrow when I'll join you as your guide," said Noaita. After the formal address by the professor and the tour guide, the students were all permitted to go into their huts and make themselves comfortable. One hour after the students settled into their huts, Professor Santos had to return to Manicore, and then proceed to the capital of Brazil where he resides.

"Thank you Professor, it's all perfect as expected," said Prof. Hendrix.

"I'll return to this village in exactly seven days from now, so be prepared for me," said Prof. Santos.

"Please, I'll be expecting you because there won't be any means of reaching you since there isn't any communication network in this village," said Prof. Hendrix. While the Professors chatted about logistics, Professor Hendrix's worry was compounded not just by the lack of access to the outside world because of the remoteness of their research location but also because there isn't any vehicle in sight in the entire village. The road is rough and rugged and the buses that brought the research team had to create their own road.

"Worry not, I'll be here with the buses to take you out of the village," said Prof. Santos.

"I also observed there isn't a single vehicle in this village," said Prof. Hendrix.

"Yeah, if you observed carefully you'll notice there are no roads except a footpath, but the buses just made their way through till we got here," said Prof. Santos. As they discuss a means of transportation that would allow them access to the outside world in case of an emergency, Professor Santos pointed to some bicycles at a distance as a way of letting Professor Hendrix know that all hope isn't lost.

The distance between Manicore and Humaita might not be much but the level of civilization between these two villages is world apart. While Manicore host some features of a town that is associated to a municipal headquarters, Humaita seems like a village in the Stone Age.

"Despite these odds, this village remains the best location for this research and the only place to achieve our objective," said Prof. Hendrix.

Moments later, Professor Santos returned to Manicore with the busses, leaving Professor Hendrix and the students behind in the Village of Humaita. The Professor returned to his students and went straight into his hut after seeing his fellow professor off, but not long after he entered his hut, he heard a knock at the door.

"Professor, can we go around the village just to feast our eyes?" asked Kelvin.

"Yes you can, tomorrow our guide will lead us into the forest," said Prof. Hendrix.

"Professor, there seems not to be a single car in this village. How do we get out of here in case of an emergency?" asked Kelvin.

"We don't hope for an emergency situation, but there are bicycles here that we can ride to Manicore to get whatever help we need," the professor assured.

CHAPTER

THREE

1st of June – First Day of the Sun

A few minutes after the professor returned to his hut after attending to Kelvin's request to go for a brief walk within the village, Kelvin went for Amanda requesting she take a walk with him.

"Baby, let's walk around and see what the village looks like," said Kelvin. While Kelvin wanted to go for a brief walk within the village, Amanda seems to have something else in mind. Funnily, the professor only granted Kelvin permission to take a look around the village, but they're now unwittingly taking a walk into the forest. "I love this trip. There's so much fun to have, we had fun in the flight, in the jungle lodge, now we're heading into the forest where I'll have to kiss you for eternity, and when we come back to the hut we'll continue our romance," said Amanda. Kelvin doesn't seem too keen on frolicking alone in the forest with Amanda, he unsurprisingly had to rush back to his friends and ask them to join them for a walk around the village.

"Let's see if others will join us, said Kelvin. "No babe, let's go in alone, just you and me, and it's going to be fun," Amanda proposed. Amanda clinged onto Kelvin pestering him continually for a romantic trip alone in the forest, but Kelvin seems keen on doing just the opposite for the fear of the unknown.

"Let's not walk alone into a forest we know nothing about," said Kelvin. He then hurtled back to the hut to get his friends on board. "Guys, we want to have a brief walk into the forest, let's just look around and come back," said Kelvin.

Interestingly, after Kelvin proposed the idea to his friends, many of them bought Kelvin's proposal, and suddenly the number of those interested in going for walk are swelling the ranks, and not long Kelvin has convinced seven of his colleagues to come with them. "Joel, let's join them, I'd love to have some fun," said Kimberly without any hesitation.

"Ok, I'm up for it, but let me get my phone," said Joel.

"I'll go with you guys, the fun won't be complete without me," said Lee. Terry and Tyler also stood up and joined but Tyler's interest in Vera hasn't diminished, and despite the dissing he got from her during their flight, he still wanted her to come with him.

"Vera, aren't you coming with us?" asked Tyler.

Vera turned her attention away from Tyler as if he didn't exist.

"I'm not up for that, and I prefer to remain cooped up indoors than go with you," said Vera. Sadly, Vera continued to give Tyler the short end of the stick and she isn't ready to take the guy serious because she finds his words to be full of hot air, enough to fly a balloon. Tyler had no choice but to crawl away, because he couldn't bear Vera's dressing down. Vera's latest comment was thought provoking for some of the guys, and it didn't take long before some of Tyler's friends nudged him to run as far as his feet could him, at least to get away from Vera. Lee on the other hand has something else in mind, enough to startle his friends.

"Oh, wait a minute," said Lee. While others waited, Lee rushed back to his hut, opened his bag, rummaged through its content and a minute later took two smoke canisters and a taser. He then returned to his friends but all the guys burst into laughter the moment he joined them armed with smoke canisters and a taser.

"What on earth are you doing with that! Are you going to war or something?" asked Joel.

"In case we need it, there used to be jaguars in these forests. Though, deep into the forest, I suppose," said Lee.

"I've asked Lee the same question, and what will these do to a roaring jaguar?" asked Kelvin. Terry is always the guy that likes cutting to the chase, and thinks the back and forth is taking too much time.

"Guys, enough of the drama, let's start going," said Terry.

Proactively, they heed to Terry's call, and immediately began their walk around the village, and it didn't take long before they fell in love with the cultural settings and even the natives who came out in their numbers to see these guests' parade around their village. After walking the length and breadth the village, and seen all there's to see, the students strayed a bit into the forest, but it is now time to return to their huts.

"Guys, we've enjoyed ourselves, it's time we get back to the village," said Kimberly.

"Kimberly is right, I think we should be heading back to the village," said Lee.

They continued at the same pace without paying heed to those suggesting they return to the village, and strayed further into the forest without a guide. They walked around, enjoying the beauty of the forest and actually had fun, until they spotted a rock from a distance.

"Guys, look at that," said Kelvin. Pointing at a rock some kilometres away, and funnily, the sight of this rock arrested their attention and kept them captive.

"But that's a rock, and why is it so red?" asked Lee.

"Hey! That's about three kilometres from our present location," said Joel.

"Three kilometres is quite some distance and we're already about four kilometres away from the village," said Tyler. Most of the students are eager to return to the village, not only because they've had enough but because their feet are tired, and also not give in to the temptation of walking another three kilometres to see this weird looking rock.

"Have you seen a rock as red as that before?" asked Kelvin.

"Of course not, though the rock is kind of strange," said Lee.

"We're here on a research expedition, and we might learn something new from this as well," said Kelvin.

"But Lee said there are jaguars in this forest, aren't we straying too far into the forest?" said Amanda.

"You guessed right, but let's see what mystery that rock holds," said Lee. Unfortunately, the voice of the few who want to see this rock more closely drowned out the voice of the many who felt they should return immediately to the village. The students had to make another three kilometres walk into the forest to reach the location of the rock, but they didn't only dip their toes into the forest, they unwittingly plunged into the deep end of the forest.

After about an hour and half of meandering through the paths in the forest, they finally got to the rock, and the students were wonderstruck as they gazed in awe at the blood mountain that is something out of the ordinary, far beyond whatever their eyes have ever seen.

"This rock is looking so red, it's even by the edge of the river," said Lee.

"This rock looks strange, and I've never seen a rock this red before," said Joel. The students were so excited to have made this discovery, at least they're on a research adventure, and this will make sense.

They then hopped from one place to another enjoying the sight of the rock and forgetting they're seven kilometres away from the remotest of civilization any human can think of.

"Coming to this rock should be counted as part of our research work because there's a lot to learn in this forest," said Tyler.

"Oh, my legs are killing me, but the trekking is worth it because I've never seen any rock like this one," said Amanda. They couldn't return without memorialising this discovery in the Amazon forest, what's best way to do that if not by taking photographs.

"At least our coming here is worth it. Guys, bring out your cameras, let's take pictures," said Kelvin.

The sun is setting, and darkness falls fast in the Amazon, yet these students were having the fun of their lives, dawdling around and taking their time to take as much photographs as possible.

"Guys, let's be quick with the pictures, so we can start going back to the camp," said Kimberly.

"I need enough pictures, my visit to this rock will be a tale I must tell," Tyler retorted.

"Guys, let's take some group pictures," Lee proposed. They all climbed the rock and took as many pictures as possible, laughing and chatting away. Even as some are urging it's time to go, Tyler still needed more photographs as a proof and trophy of this expedition. While these students were enjoying the eye popping riverside view in this forest and taking pictures to memorialise their visit, Kimberly called Joel aside for a selfie, just for two of them.

"Guys, I need to take some pictures by this river, before I leave," said Tyler.

After spending about forty-five minutes taking pictures on the rock, it's finally time to go and the students decided to find their way back to the camp, but unfortunately, their confusion began an hour later as they could no longer find their way out of the forest.

"Guys, what's happening to us? We don't seem to be finding our way back to the village," said Kelvin.

"I've noticed what you just said, but I thought it was my eyes that were deceiving me," said Terry. The confusion is now growing by the minute, and despair has now taken hold after an hour and twenty minutes of trying to find their way out as they unfortunately find themselves by the riverbank again.

"Let's look for a trail that'll help us. Sweet wrappers, shoe prints, just anything and at least we've been eating sweets and chewing gums since we entered this forest," said Joel.

"I can't find any trail, and we're deep into the forest, and who'll find us here!" Amanda exclaimed.

"I've been looking out for trails, but they seem to have been mysteriously wiped out," said Kelvin.

While the seven of them were still trying to find their way out of the Maici riverbank, darkness began to fall on them.

"It's getting dark, and how come none of us has a compass?" said Lee.

"I came with a compass, but it isn't here, it's in the camp, and I believe most of us came with one at least," said Kelvin.

"We only wanted to go for a walk, and none of us expected we would find ourselves in this mess," said Tyler. Amanda has been clinging onto Kelvin all along, but this time she isn't letting go of Kelvin's hand as darkness began to settle in.

"I'm afraid, Kelvin. I don't know what's going on," said Amanda. Joel quickly brought his faith to bear as he assured his friends.

"I'm sure God will protect us, nothing evil will happen to any of us," he said. Obviously, Joel's assurances didn't diminish the his friends concerns in any way, yet he continued to assure them he prayed before making this trip, and he's certain they will all return home in one piece.

"God, I trust You, but why did You allow us to get to this point in the first place?" asked Kimberly.

"Oh, my Kimberly, you're a Christian. Why are you sounding like this?" asked Joel. Sadly, most of the students shared Kimberly's view and supported her decision to question God for not coming to their aid. Some of the students see Joel as clinging onto a baseless religiosity, and they rebuked him for being opinionated and grabbing free hanging apples to make a case for God.

"Joel, leave Kimberly alone, she has the right to express herself because I'm equally afraid," said Lee.

The cost of these students' exuberance isn't just a slap on the wrist, it might cost them much more than an arm and a leg because coming out of this forest unscathed is now farfetched. Arguably, not in this lifetime did these students believe they would be confronted with the horror of being trapped in a forest located in the middle of nowhere.

"The light from my phone seems not to be enough, you guys should put the light in your phones on," said Tyler.

"My phone is down, the battery is gone," said Kimberly.

"I've just one bar of charge left on my phone and we need to find ways of conserving energy," said Lee.

"Let's be calm, panic will do us no good," said Joel. Anger is beginning to brew in their mist, particularly against Kelvin who persuaded them to visit the rock in the first place.

"Kelvin, I suppose, you know you're responsible for this?" asked Tyler.

"How! How can you blame this on me?" asked Kelvin. Tyler remained hopping mad at Kelvin despite Kelvin's defence.

"After some time in the forest, I suggested we all go back, but you insisted we go a bit further," Tyler insisted.

Interestingly, Amanda didn't hesitate to come to her boyfriend's rescue.

"Leave Kelvin out of this, Kelvin never forced you to wander further into the forest," she protested. Tyler stopped and flashed his light at Amanda as she clings unto her boyfriend and didn't say much, rather he complimented them.

"Oh, lovebirds, I get it," said Tyler. "Instead of this argument, we should be worried about how our Professor is feeling right now," said Joel.

"That's true, and Joel is right," said Kimberly.

Back at their huts in the village of Humaita, the professor has been worried sick about these seven students' safety, as he waited with bated breath because he's personally responsible for their safety. He has no clue of the direction they went, and neither did the students that stayed behind in the village.

"Where are these students? Don't they know they should be back by now?" said Prof. Hendrix.

"Professor, maybe they've missed their way," said Samantha.

"How can they miss their way? Are they kids?" asked Prof. Hendrix. There's already panic in the camp and the professor isn't exempted, yet he kept faith alive and hoping that his students will soon return to the village.

"The strange thing is that we can't even reach them through the phone," said Mallon.

"We're in the middle of nowhere, and there's no phone network here," replied Prof. Hendrix. The worried and scared students in the camp kept moving from one place to another, trying in desperation to see if they could get mobile phone network connection but all such efforts failed. Some natives were amazed at the manner in which the students' held up their mobile phones searching for mobile network, the students were in fact acting as if they're star gazers trying to make contact with aliens.

"I can't even reach out to the UK to inform the university authority because of the network problem," said Beata.

"Don't do that! Don't inform anyone in the UK about this, we'll search for them ourselves," said Prof. Hendrix.

"Why, Professor?" Chantell asked curiously.

"Let us avoid creating a panic situation," said Prof. Hendrix.

"Let's speak to the villagers, to see if they can help us with the search," said Johnny.

"Sure, let's do that. Please, you guys should come with me," said Prof. Hendrix. The professor and his students hurriedly made their way to seek help from the villagers, but rather than running off to the village head for help, they all made their way to the only person who will possibly understand their language and plight.

Back in the forest, there is this cacophony of sounds that makes the darkness quite eerie in a way. The students stopped and listened in, and then cringed at the sound of wolf barking at a distance. It's now about 9.00 pm and while the students were still groping in the dark, there was a sudden calm in the forest; the birds had stopped singing, the trees stopped whistling, the frogs stopped croaking and the wind stopped blowing. There was eerie silence, this silence continued for about five minutes and suddenly a rustling noise that sounded like a fast moving train began to tear through the forest and the students became terrified.

"What is going on?" asked Kelvin. They all scampered for safety and hid themselves.

"What's that? Put off your lights, do it quickly," said Joel. Weeping Amanda couldn't hold her peace any longer, as she now needs support from her Kelvin who himself is almost peeing in his pants.

"Kelvin, please hold me, I'm afraid and I don't want to die," cried Amanda.

"Shush, you'll not die, just stop talking," Kelvin said, as he tries to keep her calm in a whispering voice.

"I don't think coming to a place like this for research is a good idea," said Lee.

After about ten minutes, the intense rustling sound stopped, but the forest was still very calm and the students still remained in their position of cover, but were a bit relieved that the terrifying thrust through the forest has stopped.

"What actually made that noise?" asked Tyler.

"I don't have the slightest idea of what that could be, but I know for sure it isn't a train," said Kelvin.

"That thing must be as long as a train, though it doesn't sound like a train, and there are no train tracks here," said Lee.

"What sort of animal could that be? Please, let's just leave our lights off", said Kimberly. The absolute calm in the forest remained as the students continued to second-guess what it is that forced the forest to utterly submit to its presence.

"You all can see how quiet the forest is. Whatever animal it is, I'm certain the forest bows to its presence," said Joel.

"Then this place must be evil!" exclaimed Amanda.

"Evil is an understatement, this place is wicked," said Kelvin, as they continued to speak in a low whispering voice.

"Hey Kelvin, Amanda is afraid already, don't multiply her fears," said Joel.

"Oh, I'm sorry Amanda, just keep holding on to me," said Kelvin.

In the camp, the professor and the other students met with Noaita to inform him of the missing seven students and to ask for his help to find them.

"My visitors, where are you going this night?" asked Noaita. The professor who was already looking overwhelmed and maddened by the action of his students reached out for help from his first line of contact.

"Noaita, please, we need your help," said Prof. Hendrix. Sadly, Noaita who wasn't expecting any drama from his guests at this time of the night didn't hesitate to ask the professor what help is it he wants from him.

"Some of the students that came with me went inside the forest this afternoon, and they haven't come back," said Prof. Hendrix.

"Why did they go into the forest without a guide? Are you sure they've not climbed the blood rock?" asked Noaita. Surprised at what the 'blood rock' is all about.

"Blood rock, you said. What do you mean by blood rock?" asked Prof. Hendrix.

"It's a big rock, but located far inside the forest and if you step on it you'll miss your way, unless you're a native," said Noaita.

"How far is this blood rock you're talking about?" asked Prof. Hendrix.

"It's very far from here, it's about seven kilometres away," said Noaita. Funnily, the professor underestimated his students.

"But my students wouldn't have gone this far into the forest, they just went for a walk," said Prof. Hendrix.

"You're not with them, so you can't tell how far they've gone," said Noaita. The students with the professor began to muttering among themselves, and wondering how their colleagues could have wandered seven kilometres into the deep end of a forest they knew nothing about.

"Then I'll need your help, so we can go in search for them," said Prof. Hendrix.

"Of course not, that won't be possible," said Noaita. The professor interjected, suggesting Noaita's response lacks common sense, before asking to know why going in search of his students won't be possible.

"Today and tomorrow are days of the sun," said Noaita. Unfortunately for the professor, he had so much faith in Noaita but Noaita's dawdling disposition doesn't seem to be helpful to the professor and his students in their increasingly exasperated state of worsening confusion.

"What do you mean by that?" asked Prof. Hendrix. "Ngala-na will be coming out, and patrolling the forest," said Noaita. The mention of a creature or being patrolling the forest thrown into the mix seem to have set off the fear of impending terror in the belly of the professor and his students.

"Who's Ngala-na?" the ignorant professor asked curiously.

"She's the god of the forest," said Noaita.

While the conversation progressed, Noaita's wife, Penito, who didn't understand English language noticed from the gestures that this isn't the usual casual discourse between her husband and his guests, but one that's contentious. She then drew closer and politely joined the conversation. "What are they talking about?" asked Penito. "They want me to take them to the forest," said Noaita. "Oooh! That won't be possible, because Ngala-na will be going around the forest," said Penito. Noaita then explained further to Penito the professor's dilemma that he's pressed on all sides, yet need to rescue his students from the forest.

"Some of the students that came with him, went into the forest since afternoon and haven't come back," said Noaita. Penito held her head in surprise.

"Why did they go into the forest in days like this, without help?" asked Penito. Penito's reaction freaked the hell out of the students.

"What the hell is going on?" asked Johnny.

"Professor, these people are hiding something. I swear to God we'll burn down this village if anything happens to my friends," Collins threatened. "Professor, they seem to be hiding something from us," said Chantell.

Johnny drew closer and grabbed Noaita forcefully, moving away from mere talks into action.

"Tell us what you know. Where are you hiding our friends?" Johnny threatened.

"Stop, Johnny, stop. Let's not lose our heads, we still need him," the professor said, as he stepped in to free Noaita from Johnny's grip.

"Who else can we speak to for help?" asked the Professor.

"I know how you feel, but just be patient. They might come back tomorrow but if you go in you might not make it back," said Noaita.

It's now about 9pm and it now seems the only way out of this will be going it alone without the help of these dawdling villagers, since efforts to convince Noaita has failed.

"Professor, let's go into the forest with flashlights and guns if we can find some," said Johnny.

"Of course not, Johnny. I can't afford to increase the casualties," said Prof. Hendrix.

Back in the forest, it's now few minutes past 9pm and just when they thought that things couldn't get any weirder, the lost students suddenly noticed a bright shining light from a diamond vomited by a large snake, about a hundred meters away from their place of hiding. This increased the terror in the students as they could now see the snake clearly due to the presence of the bright light.

"What the hell is that?" asked Tyler.

"That seems like a snake," said Lee.

"Where does that light come from?" asked Kelvin.

"It seems the snake vomited it, and that's a mighty snake," said Joel. Lee's focus shifted from the beast that vomited the shinny light, to what's actually producing the light.

"It isn't just any light, it's a diamond," said Lee. Amanda continued clinging onto Kelvin in fear as she muttered that she has a phobia for snakes, but now her phobia has grown worse because this isn't just any snake.

Kelvin interjected and said he's worried about Amanda because she has a phobia for darkness, this time her trouble was exacerbated by the fact that snakes give her the creeps. Arguably, the sheer size of this snake isn't just going to give her the creeps, it left her spooked. As they scrambled through the dark, finding a foot path is now difficult yet they can't stop now, particularly when help isn't in sight.

"I'm afraid this snake is evil," said Kimberly. The students banded together, and spoke in whispers as they try to stay out of harm's way.

"Yeah, you're right, you guys noticed the sounds in the forest have resumed, after the snake vomited the diamond," said Joel.

"From record, I learnt the longest snake is less than ten meters long," said Kelvin.

"This snake is more than fourteen meters long," said Lee. The threats in the forest don't seem to go away, even as the students shifted their attention to the length of the snake, what about the presence of other wild beasts that might be strolling by.

"Please lower your voice, so we don't attract the wrath of this snake," said Joel.

This trip is quite unravelling for the students, as it moves from adventure to danger, and now to education, as Tyler said he thought stories of large snakes vomiting diamonds to help them see were only a myth, but they aren't. "Shush, look! The snake is leaving," said Amanda.

"Oh my God, the beast is leaving its diamond behind," said Kelvin.

"Where's it going?" asked Joel. "To feed, or something," said Lee.

"What if it comes upon us?" asked Tyler.

"It probably will hide close to the light, to kill any animal attracted by its light and I don't think it'll come towards us," said Lee.

"Guys, let's start praying, and I suggest we stay here and not rattle the tail of this thing," said Joel.

The professor and the students returned to their huts disappointed, worried and deflated.

"Guys, I want you all to be attentive," said Prof. Hendrix.

"This situation isn't just scary, and it's very concerning," said Johnny.

"Professor, I suggest we all stay awake, as they might come in very late," said Chantell.

"We'll continue tomorrow, though let's hope they come back tonight," said Prof. Hendrix. The professor and his students stood in front of their hut and brainstormed on the way forward. His fear about the whereabouts of his students morphed into suspicions that the villagers might also have a hand in this, possibly maybe they've been kidnapped or something. Blind trust for the villagers is now a luxury the professor can't afford. Unfortunately the professor thinks he's in control all long but he just realised he isn't.

"Professor, if they don't seem ready to help us, we should go into that forest ourselves," said Johnny.

Samantha drew closer to Vera and whispered into her ear.

"You're unusually anxious and tense about this matter, why?" asked Samantha.

"I'm worried about Tyler," said Vera, in a broken voice.

"What about the others, doesn't their safety matter to you?" Samantha prodded her further.

"I care about the safety of all the students, but Tyler told me he liked me, and I told him off," said Vera.

"If you don't like him, then you actually have nothing to worry about," said Samantha. Vera went silent for a while, she knew she didn't only tell him off, she actually shoved Tyler under the bus, and as if the words were forced out of her mouth.

"Not really, actually, I'm beginning to like him," confessed Vera.

"Then what's in your mind?" asked Samantha.

"All I needed is an opportunity to tell him, I like him too," said Vera.

"Don't worry, they'll all come back, and you'll be able to tell Tyler how much you care about him," Samantha assured Vera.

The stranded students remained hidden in the forest, as they watched the snake from a distance. After about six hours of using the diamond as bait, no prey came along; the snake crawled back into the light then swallowed the diamond and made the same rustling noise as it returned to the river.

CHAPTER

FOUR

2nd of June – Second Day of the Sun

The Professor stayed up all night and hopping against hope that his students will miraculously return to him, but that hope faded as the day breaks. Just as the day breaks, Professor Hendrix and his students rushed to Noaita's place to seek his help in the search for the students inside the forest.

"Hello Noaita, how're you?" asked the distraught professor.

"Ooh, my visitors how're you, and I hope you slept well?" asked Noaita.

"You sure know I can't sleep in our present circumstance. Please, we want you lead us into the forest," said Prof. Hendrix.

"But I told you already, yesterday and today are days of the sun, and no one enters the forest," Noaita stressed. Though, Noaita is now being perceived as a heartless person, and a man without a soul by his guests because of his refusal to go into the forest in search for the missing students. Funnily, these two days are the only days in a year the natives stay away from their forest.

"These students are my responsibility, and I can't leave them in the forest," said Prof. Hendrix.

"I understand your worries, but there's nothing anyone can do," said Noaita. Feeling frustrated from Noaita's refusal to assist with the search for his students, the distressed professor turned his attention elsewhere for succour.

"Please take me to your village head, I'll need to speak with him," said Prof. Hendrix.

"Do you think it's necessary? He'll give you the same response," said Noaita.

"I don't mind, just take me to him," the professor insisted.

"Ok, if you insist. Let's go to him," said Noaita. They left to see the village head popularly referred to as Ta-Piraha.

Back in the forest, the students were still rattled by the drama of the previous night, as they stayed put in one position, trying to stay alive until daybreak.

Obviously, the students were excited at the first gleam of dawn as it signalled to them that the horror of the previous night is over.

"Please let's do everything we can to find our way back to camp," said Amanda. When these students began this trip, they thought the lines are clear all along but they soon realised that everything has suddenly become blurred. Amanda has soon forgotten about her bucket list of romantic adventures all lined up before she set off on this trip..

"Do you know my concern?" asked Lee. "You're waiting for the fat lady to sing, I suppose, other than that, you should have no concern?" Amanda retorted.

"What's your concern?" asked Kimberly.

"I need to get hold of that diamond," said Lee.

"What? Just tell me you're joking," said Joel. While his friends are keen to remind him that total absence of fear is foolishness, Lee interjected and reminded his colleagues that he's the son of an army general and he isn't afraid, then muttered saying this is his opportunity to get rich.

"You must be silly and I can't put my girlfriend through any such risk," said Kelvin. Amanda's dream of frolicking around with her boyfriend isn't just under threat but all that has gone with the wind. She's now tight-lipped as her forest experience from the previous night meant she's glad to put her romantic dream behind just to stay alive.

"Guys, let's go to the river and freshen up. It's time we start finding our way out of this God-forsaken forest," said Joel. Lee is an adventurous nerd who likes taking everything and leaving nothing behind. But greed has suddenly taken hold of him, and this greed has just turned into a cancer and it's beginning to eat deep into his soul, as the thought of finding his way out of this forest is now trashed.

"Lee, if we want to get the diamond how do we go about it?" asked Terry. The forest has infected Lee's soul and his greed is now infecting some within the fold and stealing the diamond is now the only conversation being discussed as they all walked to the river.

"Lee, stop trying to be a hero. Ten bullets won't kill the monster you saw last night, and do you think we're more intelligent than that snake?" asked Kelvin.

"Sure, we're," said Lee. They finished freshening up and began making their way through the foot path in the forest. Terry is now poisoned by Lee's obsession to steal the diamond from the snake.

"I'm with you in this, Lee. I'm ready to go the whole hog just to get that diamond, and I'm encouraging you guys to join," said Terry. We are already cursed by this forest, and now you're planning on stealing the jewel of the forest, what makes you think we can ever come out of this?" asked Amanda.

"Calm down, Amanda. We can smoke the forest, and steal the diamond," said Lee who remained optimistic.

"Are you saying if we stay behind, you'll steal the diamond?" asked Kelvin.

"Of course yes, I'll steal the diamond, all you guys should do is hang around and watch from afar," said Lee. Amanda who was the biggest emotional casualty of the trauma of the previous night seems to be having none of Lee's gibberish, as she's intent on breaking forth from this forest. She interestingly turned to Kelvin who's her only source of succour.

"Kelvin, are you expecting me to witness exactly the same terror as last night?" asked Amanda. Joel and Kimberly are already itching to get going, as they realised that their colleagues have become overbearing and increasingly foolish. Sad to say, that Lee's surreal intention is one that could result in brouhaha among these friends, yet Lee insists that the monster of the previous night should be anything but feared. As far as Lee is concerned, his wealth, and his riches is lying idly in the belly of that beast, and he must get it out of the beast.

"I don't have time for these pranks, let's look for something we can eat?" said Joel. In a sudden twist of event, as if he just lost his senses, Kevin suddenly seem to forget about Amanda's fears and suggested the unimaginable.

"I don't mind staying another night provided Lee will be the one to steal the diamond," said Kelvin.

"You must be joking, Kelvin. Don't tell me you're up for this," said Amanda. It's now blindingly obvious to Kelvin that romance is no longer in Amanda's playpen, because the idea of a pet name for Kelvin seems forgotten. Before now she refers to him as Kev, coined from Kelvin. In his bid to persuade his colleagues to stay behind, and in his usual astute nature, Terry decided to play a game of choosing between survival and thievery.

"Guys, we're all staying behind, let's put it to a vote if any of you disagree," said Terry. Sadly, Terry unwittingly brought in forest politics as he attempts to play Russian roulette with his friends' lives at this sensitive time as a way of addressing division. This Terry's annoying enthusiasm to manage the brewing animosity within their ranks might only help Lee's course, but not his course mates.

"What about the professor? You guys know he wouldn't like this idea," said Joel. Funnily, Lee thinks otherwise as he unsurprisingly didn't hesitate to remind his colleagues that his move will add colour to the research, and the professor will gladly add their findings to his research. Joel was standing with Kimberly a few meters away from his colleagues, but became pensive as he remained silent for a while reflecting on their experience a day before. After a momentary reflection, he walked into the mist of his friends.

"Guys, something isn't right here, we were foolish yesterday and later became pensive for taking a walk too far into the forest, and suddenly we've shrugged everything off and became greedy and our greed has turned into obsession. Let's hope we don't choke on our obsession," said Joel. Terry didn't hold back his support for the heist, as he pressed on with his support for Lee. Joel interjected and suggested to his colleagues that this monster hasn't backed them into the corner in a manner that requires them to fight for their life, in a case of 'you're damned if you do and you're damned if don't.' Amanda on the other hand, thinks there's only one sensible option here, and that's to let the sleeping dog lie since the monster isn't on their path.

Even as they made their way to the village head's palace, Noaita made it clear to them that not a cat in hell's chance will the village head allow any of his subject set foot in that forest. Arguably, Noaita's comment sparked outrage as some of the students branded him a cynic of some sort, and accused him of making things up. The professor interjected immediately to calm all frayed nerves as he reminded his students that Noaita is the only link between them and these villagers, and urged them not to burn that bridge.

Following the professor's insistence, Noaita took him and his students to meet with Ta-Piraha, the village head. As expected, Ta-Piraha received them with open arms. The village head was aware of their arrival but they haven't been formally introduced, and unfortunately, they are meeting under a different circumstance.

"Noaita, please you'll be my interpreter," said Prof. Hendrix.

"Ok, I'll do that for you," said Noaita.

"Please tell your king, I need help to find my students who are in the forest," said Prof. Hendrix.

"Tell him yesterday and today are days of the sun, and my subjects don't enter the forest," said Ta-Piraha.

"Tell him, I don't know if my students are ok or not, that I must enter that forest today," Prof. Hendrix retorted.

"Tell him to be patient. From tomorrow, we'll go into the forest and we'll help him get them," said Ta-Piraha.

"What if they're in danger, sick, dead, or something? Tell him I can't wait here and do nothing," replied Prof. Hendrix.

"Ok, tell him to wait. Let the chief priest consult the oracle to see if they're alive," said Ta-Piraha. The village head sent for the chief priest and not long the chief priest walked into the palace. While the professor remained worried sick that his students run the risk of being devoured by a jaguar, the chief priest put his mind to rest as he informed the professor that they should only be worried about Ngala-na and not about some wild animal devouring his students. The Chief Priest's remark riled the professor and his students further as he reminded them that even the jaguars aren't immune to Ngala-na, stressing that the forest stays still and even the wild beasts' hides away whenever Ngala-na roams the forest. The Chief Priest then began some traditional semantics, but sadly, the students can't wait any longer as they're already incensed and irritated by these unnecessary protocols, and Johnny who's always the feisty one isn't having any of it.

"Professor, we don't have time for this," said Johnny.

"Johnny, wait, let's give them some minutes," said Prof. Hendrix. After making some incantations and consultations, the chief priest gave them his findings. "They're all fine," said the Chief Priest.

"Noaita, please ask him if he's very sure of what he just said?" asked Prof. Hendrix. Noaita turned to the Chief Priest.

"He said I should ask you, if you're sure of what you just said," asked Noaita.

"Yes I'm sure, and they just finished washing up themselves in the Maici River," said the Chief Priest.

"Oh, to hear they're fine gives me some relief," said Prof. Hendrix.

The students were surprised at their atheist professor's sudden faith in the Chief Priest.

"Don't tell me you believe in this traditional crap, professor," said Johnny.

"Tell him my students and I will be going inside that forest to look for the missing students," said Prof. Hendrix. The professor and his students stood up and left the palace, leaving the village head and chief priest behind. Noaita ran after the professor to warn him not to dare into the forest.

"Don't do that, it's not good," said Noaita.

"Please don't even try to stop me, but I still need you to help me with a gun, a spear or something," said Prof. Hendrix.

"Do you really need a gun?" asked Noaita.

"Of course, I do, but I'll pay you for it and I will give you good money." The professor promised.

"Ok, I'll help you with a gun, though it's not a good idea," said Noaita. Worried about the warnings of the villagers and the unknown fate that awaits them in the forest, Vera turned to her colleagues.

"Professor, I don't think it's a good idea for the whole lot of us to go into the forest, what if we suffer the same fate?" asked Vera. The professor stopped to make sense of Vera's comment.

"Noaita, I need two bicycles as well," said Prof. Hendrix.

"Please, as you go into the forest, stay away from the blood rock, though it's far into the forest," Noaita warned.

"Please, how does this rock look?" asked Vera. "The rock is big, and red, if you see it you'll know," said Noaita.

Back in the forest, after washing up at the river, the students made their way through the forest and settled for breakfast as they nourished themselves by gathering some wild fruits they think are edible.

"Oh, I like the taste of these fruits," said Joel.

"There's no need worrying ourselves about going back to the camp when we've got a diamond to collect," said Lee.

"Going back to the village is my priority," said Amanda.

"I suggest we go back to the village, while those interested in the diamond heist can come back at night to drink the kool-aid," said Kelvin, whose interest is now his girlfriend's safety.

"That diamond could change our lives, including that of Professor Hendrix," said Terry.

"Professor Hendrix is already made, he doesn't need your diamond and let's not make his life miserable," said Kimberly.

Lee continues to moralise the heist, as he insists that Professor Hendrix can use the proceeds to fund even bigger research projects. "You guys should store some fruits in your pockets, and let's start finding our way to the village," said Joel.

Not long afterwards, they spotted Africanized honeybees known to be the most aggressive bee species. The honey was mouth wateringly enticing for the hungry students who saw this as an opportunity to change their diet from wild fruits to something more refreshingly sweet, just that they would have to go through the honey bees to get to the honey.

The hive was high up on the tree, and the hungry student couldn't bear not to have a taste of the honey, but none will dare disturb this bee hive.

Lee who is known for taking all he can get and leaving nothing behind decided that if no one can, he'll dare the bees and steal their honey. His colleagues immediately kept their distance to avoid incurring the wrath of these bees that would eventually become angry when disturbed. Lee turned around and moved the opposite direction as he advanced towards the bee hive, while his friends watched with a bated breath.

Lee was in high spirit, he immediately tied some leaves around his head, looking like a warrior of one of the Amazon tribe. He then fearlessly climbed the tree and reached high up the tree to the amazement of his course mates, even as the bees were all over him. Amazingly, the painful sting of these bees didn't stop Lee as he shook the trees and contended for the honey with the bees, and not long he got the honey comb. The honey came at a price, as his swollen face bears the stings from the bees by the time he got down from the tree. Lee's triumphant return didn't go unnoticed as the guys began chanting support for Lee, this time they did it lustily and loudly, forgetting about their troubles for a moment. Interestingly, the honey didn't last five minutes after Lee got down from the tree as his hungry course mates rushed to get their share of the honey.

As they finished eating their honey, Terry needed something to wipe his hands and after looking around and found nothing, he suddenly realised Joel has a book he'd held so tight to himself since they walked into the forest.

"Hey Joel, please give me a few sheets from your book to wipe my hands," said Terry.

"What! No way, this is a bible and not just any book," Joel retorted.

"Of course I know that's a bible, but we're in the middle of nowhere, and I don't think you'll have a need for it," said Terry.

"I'll always have a need for it until I take my last breath, but I don't mind giving my shirt but not my bible," said Joel.

"Those of you who want to get the diamond can wait behind," said Kelvin. Five of the students started making their way to the village leaving Lee and Terry behind. Lee ran after them, "I thought we were a team, don't do this," Lee pleads.

"Lee, you're sounding psychotic, and I don't like it, we could die here if we aren't careful," said Amanda. Lee and Terry decided to join their uncooperative colleagues to make their way to the village, but after about thirty minutes of walking in the forest path.

"Guys, I don't think we're on the right path," said Kimberly.

"How come you know we're on the wrong path, and if you know the right path, how come we're here?" asked Lee.

"Let's try to retrace how we got here, maybe we'll be able to find our way out of this forest," said Joel. "That snake mustn't meet us in this forest tonight," said Amanda.

Noaita needed to give Professor Hendrix a double-barrel gun as he and the students prepared to enter the forest. It's obvious to all that Noaita was taken over by his emotions for the professor and his students, he then rushed to Ta-Piraha, the village head, to see if he could defy their tradition and send some of his subjects to assist Professor Hendrix in the search for his missing students.

"My king, isn't there any way we can give help these people?" Noaita asked, speaking Guajiro.

"Noaita, I'm very disappointed in you, because you know today is a day of the sun," Ta-Piraha retorted.

"My king, I'm sorry, it's just that, I'm overwhelmed with worries for our guests' safety," said Noaita.

"I'm worried about their safety too and if by the end of today the students aren't found, I wouldn't mind sending the entire village to assist them," said Ta-Piraha. This village head isn't known for tip toeing around the truth, and that isn't about to change now.

Noaita know he risks being perceived as a man without regard for the tradition of his people, he decided to thread with caution and quickly reference his earlier advice for his guests. Unfortunately, Noaita's position in this whole drama is likened to a rose between two thorns.

"I also told them that yesterday and today are days of the sun, but the situation has now worsened," said Noaita.

"Don't worry, I'll give whatever help necessary by tomorrow," promised Ta-Piraha.

"Ok my king, thank you," said Noaita. As Noaita turns to leave, Ta-Piraha understands that he's overwhelmed by emotion and felt the need to give him a piece of advice.

"Noaita, please don't enter that forest today, I know you're worried but be patient," advised Ta-Piraha.

"Ok, thank you my king," said Noaita.

Moments later, Noaita gave Professor Hendrix a gun and a spear as promised.

"Thank you, my friend," said Prof. Hendrix.

"I just came from the palace," said Noaita.

"What about it?" asked Prof. Hendrix.

"I asked the king to put our tradition aside and help you with the search," said Noaita. The anxious professor listened curiously to what Noaita had to say as his ears itches for good news.

"Did he agree to help?" asked Prof. Hendrix.

"No, he insisted that none of us can go into the forest, until tomorrow," said Noaita.

"You've tried in your own little way and I thank you for your help," said Prof. Hendrix.

"He promised to send the entire village into the forest to help with the search if you don't find them today," said Noaita. The professor didn't find the Village head's promises to be in anyway comforting because sending an infantry battalion for the search won't do the professor any good if his students died before the search commences, the professor doesn't have the luxury of time, and had to go it alone without the help of the natives.

"There wouldn't be need for that, because I won't come back if I don't find them," said Prof. Hendrix.

"Ok, I wish you luck," said Noaita as he turned around and left. Professor Hendrix doesn't just want to walk into this forest without a plan. He assembled his students to discuss the way forward on how to go about the search.

"Which of you can shoot a gun?" asked Prof. Hendrix. "I'm a good shooter, my dad is a farmer, I used to kill badgers with his gun," said Johnny.

"Why did you ask Noaita for bicycles?" asked Vera.

"Mallon and Collins will ride these bicycles to Manicore to make contact with the university authority in the United Kingdom in case things go south," said Prof. Hendrix.

"Professor, do we wait for them to return from Manicore before we enter the forest?" asked Samantha.

"The rest of us will go into the forest, I'll hold my pistol and Johnny will have the other gun, and Christian will have the spear," said Prof. Hendrix. The ladies seem to be left out from bearing arms in the professor's plan.

"What about us, Professor! What'll we use to protect ourselves?" asked Vera.

"Don't worry, this is about teamwork and I'm responsible for the safety of all of you," said Prof. Hendrix. Everyone must eventually become a team player if success must be recorded, but that doesn't prevent the ladies from fighting sexism wherever it rears its ugly head, yet cool heads are necessary to help them return home in one piece, and what the professor needs right now is anything but a gender debate.

"Professor, what message do we pass across to the university authority?" asked Mallon.

"Just tell the university authority everything you know, but don't inform any of the students' parents," the professor advised.

"Why, Professor?" asked Collins.

"To avoid panic, and I don't want the news headlines to be about us for now," said Prof. Hendrix. The professor has more than just mere news headlines to worry about, and keeping eavesdropping journalists at bay might be a little of a concern he doesn't want to jettison.

"When do we start going?" asked Vera.

"Make sure you take some food, something like snacks, or just anything you can eat, if the need arises," said Prof. Hendrix.

"Does that include us?" asked Mallon.

"Yes Mallon, we're leaving in the next few minutes, but I'll want Collins and Mallon to leave first," said Prof. Hendrix. A few minutes after getting themselves together, Collins and Mallon hurriedly made their way for Manicore. For them, it's an urgent trip, but also an opportunity to ride the rugged path of the Amazon.

"Do we need to ask for the police?" asked Mallon.

"Get as much help as you can and if possible inform the police in Manicore, peradventure we go into the forest and the unexpected happens," said Prof. Hendrix.

Moments after the help party left, the search party entered into the forest in search for the missing seven students. The professor painstakingly went through the plans with his students with a fine tooth comb. Yet, everything seems to quickly fall apart like a pack of cards before their eyes because as Collins and Mallon pass through the village of Parana on their way to Manicore, they were accosted by a group of natives who stopped them and held them captive.

"Where are you from?" these group of natives chorused, speaking Guajiro.

"Hey, hey, stop! We're going to Manicore," said Collins.

"What are you doing in our village?" the natives chorused again. Sadly, either side doesn't understand what the other side is saying, and as far as language remains a barrier, all that was said is just sound and gibberish. This trip to Manicore has suddenly gone pear-shaped, with this sense of foreboding that they're in for a shock.

"Collins, what are these people trying to do to us?" asked Mallon, who's already distraught.

Collins and Mallon watched in dismay as these mean and raffish natives of Parana were speaking among themselves.

"These people are thieves, let's take them to the village head" the natives said among themselves and agreed.

"Stop this, do you understand English language? We're going to Manicore," said Mallon. Unfortunately, these natives don't understand the English language and Mallon and Collins don't understand Guajiro either.

"Mallon, just calm down, try to see if your phone can receive a signal," said Collins. While the natives marched Collins and Mallon in a frenzied and out-of-controlled manner to their village head, Mallon secretly brought out his phone to see if he could get network signal. After all, they're now some kilometres closer to some sort civilization than what it is like in the village of Humaita, but sadly, there wasn't any mobile network. "Collins, there isn't a signal, the possibility of making a phone call is now defeated," said Mallon.

After an hour of intense pandemonium, the natives marched Mallon and Collins to the palace and brought them before their village head in Parana.

"Where did you find them?" the village head asked his subjects. "We found them on the path that leads to Manicore," said his subjects.

"These aren't the ones that stole the bronze face of our masquerade five years ago, yet they can't be trusted," said the village head. Frustrated by their inability to communicate with the village head, Collins became agitated, but his agitation means nothing to these irate villagers who overpowered them and kept them still.

"What gibberish are these folks saying? We don't understand what you're saying," Collins retorted.

"Can you speak English language?" asked Mallon, who looks on helplessly as the villagers held them down while the village head decides their fate.

"Why are you holding us here? We're going somewhere," said Mallon. In an attempt to give these two foreigners a listening ear and fair judgement, the village head sent for one of his subjects who understand the English language.

"Go and get me Kamti, he understands their language, he interpreted for the ones that came here five years ago," said the village head. The urgency to get to Manicore could not keep Collins silent as he continued to echo the same words.

"Please, we're going to Manicore and we're in a hurry, just let us go," said Collins. Mallon had no choice but to advise Collins of the reality on ground.

"They seem not to understand English," said Mallon. Unfortunately, the messenger sent to fetch Kamti returned and informed the village head that Kamti has gone to farm, this threw a spanner in the works for Collins and Mallon as their only hope for effective communication is now dashed.

Back in the village of Humaita, Professor Hendrix and the remaining six students have entered into the forest in search of the missing seven students, and they've been inside the forest for about three hours without result. There's also a need to tread cautiously so as not to suffer the same fate as the seven students who went missing inside the forest.

"Ensure you leave landmarks as we go, so that we can use them to retrace our steps on our way back," said Prof. Hendrix.

"Professor, what sort of landmarks are you talking about?" asked Christian.

"Use the cutlass to trim branches off trees and leaves but leave as many marks as you can. Keep looking out and screaming their names," said Prof. Hendrix. The students and their professor continued combing the forest and screaming as they go along.

"Lee, Joel, Amanda! Where are you?" Christian screamed.

"Is anyone out there?" Beata screamed.

"Tyler, Lee, Amanda! Where are you?" Vera screamed.

"Keep screaming, all of you, look out for litter from them, anything," said Prof. Hendrix.

"What kind of litter are you talking about?" asked Johnny. "Sweet wrappers or anything that can be linked to them, I can't leave this forest without them," said Prof. Hendrix. After walking a few kilometres into the forest, Christian was surprise at the sight of a conspicuously strange looking bloody rock at a distance. "Professor, look at that," said Christian. "Is that the blood rock they're talking about?" asked Johnny.

"That must be the rock Noaita talked about, let's go towards the rock," proposed Prof. Hendrix. As they cautiously approached the rock, Vera saw some trail left by her colleagues.

"Professor, look at these," said Vera.

"These must be their shoe prints," said Johnny.

"Yes, they were here but none of you should step on the rock," the professor warned. They avoided stepping on the rock, and as far as they're concerned this rock is a plague that must be avoided at all cost. They then walked around it to see if there's a path that leads to the missing students.

"Let's just keep looking around for more trails," said Christian. "Let's go around the rock to check for more trails," said Prof. Hendrix. Unfortunately for the search party, the trails seem to have suddenly disappeared and the hysteria from the trail went cold immediately and everything has now returned to square one.

"Professor, the trail seems to have suddenly disappeared," said Johnny. They however continued with their search, meandering through the dense vegetation of the Amazon forest. After spending a few hours in the forest, the students are now famished and needed to snack on something.

"Professor, we're hungry, and we need to eat something," said Samantha.

"Bring those snacks and drinks out, let's eat, and rest a bit and continue the search," replied Prof. Hendrix.

"Thank you," said Samantha. They looked for somewhere to sit and rested their feet as they ate their snacks.

Meanwhile, the missing seven found themselves circling the forest, still unable to find their way despite all efforts to retrace their steps.

"We've been patrolling this forest for about five hours today, yet there seems not to be any headway," said Lee.

"Let's not faint or lose hope, we should continue trying," said Joel.

"Is it possible for us to make something like a whistle that we can use to make our presence known in case we're being searched for?" asked Tyler.

"See what you've done to us, Kelvin," Kimberly retorted.

Emotions are beginning to run high as the blame game and finger pointing began to take over their conversation, and their inability to make headway is taking a toll and making some to lose their cool.

"What do you mean by that?" asked Amanda.

"We never wanted to go this far into the forest but Kelvin pushed us into doing this," said Kimberly.

"I suggest we stop and pray for God's help because I believe there's a spell in this forest, we may have lost our senses," said Joel. Lee doesn't believe in the idea of a divine being in the first place and as for Lee, life is que sera-sera, whatever will be, will be.

"If your God is this good, why then did he allow us to be in this mess in the first place?" asked Lee. Joel insisted they have been patrolling this forest since morning, and soon it'll go dark again, he then urged his friends to turn to payer as the only available option left.

"If it goes dark again, then it'll be an opportunity to lay my hands on that diamond," said Lee. Unsurprisingly, Lee is an optimist who radiates positivity, but his optimism might not be infectious enough to make his friends buy into the idea of a heist, because the confusion is now taking its toll on the missing students as all effort to make their way out of the forest seem to have largly failed.

"Do you guys expect that we should continue walking this forest in this manner?" asked Kelvin. Worried that just walking the forest alone without making some noise to attract people who might be searching for them isn't yielding any result. Kelvin constructed something that looked like a whistle and handed it to Tyler.

"Try this," said Kelvin. Tyler tried to blow the instrument but it wasn't blowing properly.

"Can you improve on this?" asked Tyler.

"My worry is how Professor Hendrix is feeling right now about our disappearance," said Joel.

"It's better you bother about yourself and not the professor, you're lost and he isn't," said Lee. After efforts to improve the whistle failed, the only option left is for them to use their voices to call for help.

"Please, let's keep screaming and maybe someone will hear us, anybody there?" Kelvin screamed.

"Help! Anybody here, please help us," Amanda screamed. They continued screaming as they moved around the forest trying to find their way but no one heard them. Worried that the night might fall upon them again in the forest, Joel encouraged his colleagues to conserve the energy in their phones in case darkness falls on them again.

"Guys, no more playing of games with our phones in case we need it," said Joel.

"But some of us can't use our phones because the battery is already gone," said Kelvin. "Joel is right, it'll be wise if we preserve whatever power is left in our phones," said Kimberly.

"If we can't find our way, I suggest we stay put at the very spot we stayed last night, so that we don't find ourselves on that snake's path," said Tyler.

Back in the village of Parana, Kamti returned from his farm hours later, and made his way to the palace as he answers the call of the village head that sent for him earlier.

"Kamti, I know you understand their language, so I want you to interpret for them," said the village head.

"Ok, I'll be glad to offer this service," said Kamti. The village head walked with Kamti to the holding cell where Collins and Mallon were kept, and pointed to Collins.

"Tell him I'm holding them because I don't trust them," said the village head.

"Why is he holding us, and what offence have we committed?" asked Collins.

"Tell him some of his people stole the bronze head of our masquerade five year ago," said the village head.

"Please ask him if we're the ones that stole his bronze head?" asked Collins.

"Tell him they aren't the ones that committed the offence but I just don't trust them around my village," said the village head. Mallon couldn't hold his peace and wants to add his voice to Collins' plea for their release, particularly now that there's someone that understands the English language.

"Tell him, why then should he hold us responsible for an offence committed by other people?" asked Mallon.

"Tell him I welcomed his people five years ago, but they betrayed my hospitality," said the village head. This village head's hesitation reflects his deep seated animosity and indignation with foreigners. His conscience wasn't at all pricked even as he meted this punishment in a transfer of aggression on these supposedly innocent young men on their way to Manicore for a life saving assignment.

"Tell him, we're in a hurry, and we must be in Manicore to send a message home," said Collins.

"Tell him I'm keeping them here until I'm sure of their mission in this village," said the village head.

"Please don't do this," said Collins as he aggressively banged the bamboo gate of his cell. Mallon had to advise Collins to calm down because he can't fight his way out this. Sadly, the village head seems not to give a monkey's about their mission and all effort to persuade him fell on deaf ears as he remains a big bluffer.

"I'm sorry, my king said you aren't going anywhere," said Kamti.

"Why can't you beg for us? Please help us," Collins pleads. Kamti spent a few minutes speaking Guajiro with his village head, pleading for the release of Collins and Mallon since locking them up for the sins of others will mean a blatant miscarriage of justice. Unfortunately, Kamti's plea didn't do much either. He then turned to Collins and said he has tried to let the village head understand but he refused. Moments later, the village head left, while Collins and Mallon remained locked up in a cell.

Collins paced up and down furiously banging the gate of his cell continually until his fists failed him, and he watched helplessly as the village head and Kamti walked away and out of sight.

"Let us out, we didn't steal your bronze head," Collins screamed.

"Oh my God, this is a research expedition gone bad!" exclaimed Mallon.

Hours later, the sun is beginning to set and darkness will soon fall in the forest. The missing seven students have not been able to find their way out of the forest and the Professor's search party haven't located them either. Funnily, the screams from either side didn't get through, and this research expedition is now turning fast into a multi-headed hydra with the multiple failures recorded so far. The confusion swells as the missing students felt betrayed by their professor whom they felt should've searched for them but failed to do so.

"Why's it that nobody even searched for us?" asked Amanda.

"I'm disappointed in Professor Hendrix, he brought us to this village and we went missing, yet he didn't make any effort to search for us," said Kelvin.

"How would you know if they themselves haven't gone missing in their attempt to find us?" asked Joel.

"I'm beginning to be worried," said Lee.

"Why're you worried, Lee? I suppose, it's because even if you steal the diamond, there isn't a way of escape out of the forest," asked Terry.

"This is very strange, why aren't we able to identify how we got here in the first place?" asked Tyler. The missing students continued to wander around in the forest, trying as hard as they could to make their way out of the forest, but darkness falls fast in the Amazon forest once the sun sets. "It's already getting dark, and I don't want that snake to meet me in this forest this night," said Kimberly worryingly.

"Of all the forests in the world, how come Professor Hendrix brought us to a place like this?" asked Kelvin.

"Please guys, let's begin to pray. If our knowledge can't show us the way out, maybe God will help us," Joel proposed. After all effort has failed, the idea of prayer seems to make some sense at this point as the limitation in their wisdom is now glaringly obvious to them.

"Joel, please just continue to pray for us," said Tyler.

"I want to sit down, my feet are tired and sore from walking all day," said Amanda.

"It's already getting dark and sitting down won't do us any good," said Kelvin.

"Let's trace that rock; maybe from there we'll be able to find out how we got to the rock yesterday," said Lee.

"What rock, the red rock by the river?" asked Kelvin.

"Yeah, it was from that point we missed our way yesterday," said Joel. Interestingly, day light is now a luxury these students don't have particularly now that the sunset is a few hours old, implying that darkness is now in the horizon. They dreaded walking back to the blood rock that sits just by the Maici river, kilometres away at this time of the evening because it isn't the best of ideas.

"I hope you remember that it was close to that rock, that the snake came out of the river," said Joel.

"I know, but what do we do? Instead of complaining we should continue trying," said Lee. Joel isn't giving up yet, but trying mustn't mean dawdling in the path of Ngala-na. Yesterday was a lucky escape as the students serendipitously found themselves some distance away from the path of this monster when it came tearing through the forest.

"Do you remember that we returned to that rock about three times yesterday, and yet couldn't find our way?" asked Amanda. Terry has something else in mind Ønsad Lee is now in his focus after a first-hand experience of Lee's tenacity in getting whatever he sets his sight on.

It's not the size of the dog in the fight, but the size of the fight in the dog is what matter, and after observing the fight in Lee as he contended for the honey with the bees, Terry concluded that Lee is a man whose bluff he can't call. He now has no choice but buy into Lee's dream of a diamond heist. With Terry's focus now on Lee, he suddenly told him he has a question for him.

"Yeah, go on, ask your question," said Lee.

"No, it's a one-on-one, this is personal stuff," said Terry. Lee stepped aside for a tete-a-tete with Terry, as other students expressed prejudice over their secret talks.

"Are you guys into some factional conspiracy or what?" asked Joel. "We don't need secrets in times like this," Kimberly retorted.

"No, guys you're all safe and you've got nothing to worry about," said Terry.

"Leave them to do their thing; they've the right to their privacy," Kelvin retorted.

Funnily, they both spent minutes together chatting about stuff but left out the elephant in the room, even when the elephant was right there staring at them in the face. Even the soft spoken among the ladies are divided and are unable to form a pink brigade to call these guys into order, and their exuberance didn't allow some of the students to remain passive as they just couldn't spectate alone.

Terry is known for finishing fights he didn't start, and he's about to buy this fight over, as he called Lee aside to inquire of his strategy on the heist.

"What's it, Terry?" asked Lee, after a momentary silence.

"Lee, I'm just concerned about the snake," said Terry.

"What about it? asked Lee.

"Are you really sure you want to do this?" asked Terry. Lee's contest with the honeybees was a watershed moment that got Terry more interested in buoying up Lee's desire for the diamond. Terry understands for sure that his colleagues might not be pleased with this move, as some within the group already finds him insufferable because they perceive him as someone who stirs the pond for his personal aggrandizement.

"Of course, I do. That's only if the snake comes back tonight," said Lee. It's now time to move from mere imagination to action, and Lee has to put those thoughts, imagination and even careless comments into a plan. Despite showing his unflinching support for the diamond heist hours earlier, Terry's heart is beginning to fail him. The reality of the danger of such bravery is beginning to dawn on Terry as they might end up in the belly of the snake as its dinner.

"Lee, this isn't a pantomime, this is real life danger," said Terry.

"I know," said Lee. "Then what's your strategy and how do you intend to achieve your plan?" asked Terry. Lee laid bare his plan before Terry to enable proper assessment of the viability of the plan, but funnily, things could get awkward once the point of no return is crossed, because even in real life things don't always go as planned.

"Hmm, I'll first release the smoke canisters to smoke the area, and then I'll use my taser to send an electric shock onto the snake if it comes fighting" said Lee.

"That's a perfect strategy, but do you have the heart to see it through?" asked Terry. For what it's worth, Terry considered the strategy to be a good one yet cautioned that good plans sometimes fail, and not to talk of dealing with an unpredictably cunning and wicked creature that enjoys the respect of the entire forest. He's concerned that things could quickly go south even before the action begins. Terry then reminded Lee that the snake isn't just any other snake, but a forest monster. "How do you mean? Of course, I want to see it through! If not, why not?" asked Lee.

"Do you know why I said that, Lee?" asked Terry.

"Why?" Lee asked in surprise. "Once you come close to the diamond and the snake sights you, then there will be no turning back, you either fight to the death trying to destroy the snake or the snake will kill you," said Terry.

"Ok, you're right, once I blow my cover the snake becomes an enemy, and you either kill your enemy or your enemy kills you," said Lee. After brainstorming on the pros and cons of pulling a stunt as big as this, Terry and Lee agreed that the trophy is worth the risk, but remained mum as they returned to their course mates.

"Yes, that's it, let's join the others," said Terry.

"Ok manager, you're now my manager," said Lee. They returned and joined the others after hatching and concluding on their planned heist.

It was about 6.30pm, and darkness has fallen in the forest. The professor and the students with him couldn't find the missing seven students and decided to return to the village in frustration. While the missing seven couldn't find their way out of the forest and remained in the forest, Mallon and Collins remained locked up in cell in the village of Parana.

Darkness has fallen and it's now night on the second day in the village after the professor and the students returned from the forest. The professor's despair was exacerbated after realising Collins and Mallon hasn't returned from Manicore.

"Why haven't Mallon and Collins returned to from Manicore?" asked Prof. Hendrix.

"Maybe they decided to stay back in Manicore," said Vera.

"Why should they do that? We need to know what the feedback is," said the worried Prof. Hendrix. The communication gap has become menacing for the professor and his students who remained in the dark as to the whereabouts of the missing seven, and also for Collins and Mallon who have chosen to stay behind in Manicore.

"The funny thing about this is that we can't get Collins and Mallon on the phone and they can't reach us either," said Christian.

"Why should Collins and Mallon stay back at Manicore? I need all the help available out there," Prof. Hendrix retorted.

"Maybe the university authority is sending help and requested them to wait," said Samantha. Now that the professor has recorded failures on all sides, he now needs to reason fast on the way forward, as time is now of the essence.

"Professor, what do we do next?" asked Johnny.

"Let's meet Noaita, to let him know we've been unable to find them," said Prof. Hendrix.

"Are you going to request him to join us back to the forest this night?" asked Christian.

"Whatever request I'm making will be against tomorrow morning. I hope these students are safe wherever they are," said Prof. Hendrix.

Moments after their brief deliberations, Professor Hendrix and his students left their huts and made their way to Noaita's place. Sadly, the news of the missing students is now the only news in the village of Humaita, and natives are overwhelmed by the professor's debacle. Moments later they met with Noaita to seek help with finding his students that night as they returned from the forest.

"Hey, my visitors, you're back and were you able to find them?" asked Noaita.

"Yes, we're back, but we couldn't find them and we'll need your help tomorrow," pleads Prof. Hendrix.

"Did you see the blood rock we talked about?" asked Noaita. "Yeah, it's like they climbed the rock, because I saw their shoe prints around the rock," said Prof. Hendrix.

"I think that's the reason they missed their way," said Noaita. While they stood and had their conversations, Noaita showed the professor and his students a bench for them to sit and rest their tired feet.

"But we'll need your help to locate them. I just hope they're safe," said Prof. Hendrix.

"Ok, that won't be a problem. Today's the last day of the sun, so there won't be any problem," Noaita assured the professor and his students.

"Can we get more people to join us?" asked Prof. Hendrix. The myth surrounding the blood rock means there's a mystic side to this forest, and who best to find what's lost in this forest if not those who owned the forest.

"Ta-Piraha promised to help you with as many people as you want, to help in the search," said Noaita.

"You mean your village head has agreed to give us help?" asked Prof. Hendrix.

"Of course, yes, let's go to him and tell him we'll need his help tomorrow," Noaita proposed.

Noaita took the professor to Ta-Piraha, who was eating his dinner at the time they walked into the palace, but the village head who also considers speaking while eating as a bad manner couldn't hold back but ask about the welfare of the missing students.

"Noaita, how did it go and was he able to find the students?" asked Ta-Piraha.

"No, my king, they couldn't find them. That's why he's here," said Noaita. "I told them to wait till tomorrow and I'll help them, but they refused," said Ta-Piraha. Ta-Piraha then stopped eating his dinner and drew closer to where they were seated. His disposition is more encouraging this time as he intends to assume responsibility by taking charge for the search and rescue of the students.

"That's why they're here, and they'll need your help tomorrow," said Noaita.

"Ok, I'll give him twenty hunters tomorrow to help with the search and you can also join them, so you'll be their interpreter inside the forest," said Ta-Piraha.

"Noaita, what did he say?" asked Prof. Hendrix.

"He said he'll give you twenty hunters tomorrow to help with the search," said Noaita.

"Please tell him, I'll be here very early tomorrow morning," said Prof. Hendrix.

"Ok. Don't worry, the hunters know the forest very well, and they'll find your students," Ta-Piraha assured the professor.

"That'll be good, I'll now go back to our huts to see if the boys I sent to Manicore are back," said Prof. Hendrix.

That same night, it's time for Collins and Mallon to have their dinner while still locked up in their holding cell in the village of Parana.

"My friends, how're you?" asked Kamti.

"Who's your friend? Don't ever call me that," warned Collins. Kamti wasn't swayed by Collins feisty response but continued in his cheerful manner as he tried as much as he can to tone down the tension and keep the ambience a bit friendly.

"We brought you food and I know you must be hungry," said Kamti. Mallon isn't having any of these platitudes from Kamti who understands English and should be on their side.

"Just get us out of here, we don't need your food, you savages," said Mallon.

"Why did you call us that? I'm just being nice to you but you seem to be overstepping your boundary," said Kamti. Collins understands that turning up the heat on Kamti who's their only source of hope doesn't do them any good, at least a little charm might be necessary to keep Kamti on their side.

"I know you're being nice to us, please get us out of here. We were supposed to be in Manicore," said Collins.

"Keeping us here for no reason makes you people savages," said Mallon.

"No, your people came to our village five years ago, and we welcomed them whole heartedly, but they betrayed us and stole something we hold dear in this village," said Kamti.

"How do you even know they're the ones who stole your bronze head, as you call it?" asked Mallon.

"Because I was the one that acted as their interpreter five years ago, and my people showed them so much love, but they betrayed us," said Kamti. Collins now decides it time to go on a charm offensive, at least to win Kamti who could advocate for them before the village head.

"Please, what's your name?" asked Collins.

"My name is Kamti," he said.

"Just get us out of here, we're innocent," said Mallon. Collins quickly urged Mallon to drop the nagging and tone things down, he then turned to Kamti.

"Please, we'll need your help," said Collins. Now that the blame game is over, their conversation became more cordial as Kamti gave them a listening ear.

"Ok, what help do you want?" asked Kamti. "Please help us speak to your king or whatever you call him. Let him understand we're innocent," said Collins.

"Ok, I'll speak on your behalf to our king but that'll be tomorrow morning," said Kamti.

"Why tomorrow morning and not this night?" asked Mallon.

"It's already dark and we don't go to our king when he's either asleep or about to go to bed, except it's something that can't wait," said Kamti. The travails of these two prisoners didn't count among the list of emergencies that deserves the village head's attention at night. Yet, these two students think their ordeal counts as one deserving an urgent attention.

"He's a man like you, and do you have to regard him this much?" asked Mallon. Kamti was a teacher in Manicore and has a fair degree of exposure to world affairs, which makes it easy to draw unflattering comparism of what the norm is and how traditional leaders are held in high esteem.

"You're from England, aren't you? I watch how you regard your queen on TV, why shouldn't we regard ours?" asked Kamti.

"Kamti, don't worry about the food, take it back," said Mallon.

"Why? You don't have to remain hungry, at least eat something," Kamti said as he encouraged the prisoners.

"Don't worry, Kamti. Take the food back and help us talk to your king tomorrow morning," said Collins. Unfortunately, they're famished, yet lack appetite for food. This time Collins and Mallon are in sync concerning the food because their primary concern is their freedom and not food.

"Ok, I'll do my best for you," Kamti promised, as left with the food.

Darkness has actually fallen on the forest and the missing have been unable to find their way out of the forest to the village of Humaita. Pitch black darkness has taken over the night in the forest, and Amanda on the other hand has been sobbing uncontrollably even as her foot hurts.

"Kev, I don't want to die in this forest, I don't know what's happening to us," cried Amanda.

"Calm down, babe, at least we're all still alive. We won't die tonight, I promise you," said Kelvin.

This whole research adventure that started as straightforward as hell has suddenly been shrouded in ambiguity. Amanda's perception of this research expedition as some sort of Disneyland trip makes her the person hit the hardest. She suddenly reflected on her excitement days back in Manicore when she was telling Kelvin about the plenty fun awaiting them in this research expedition, sadly the reality on ground is a far cry from her expectation.

This time all the fun and the spirit of the carnival they enjoyed just days ago in Manicore is now quickly forgotten. In for a penny, in for a pound, this is the case for these students now faced with the true cost of freedom in the Amazon Forest.

Joel brought out his bible and held it tight to his chest as he continued to pray. "Guys, please pray as much as you can," said Joel.

"Joel, why're you fidgeting? We need to be strong in times like this, at least for each other," said Terry. Kimberly picked offence at Terry's supposed strong man's posture in the mist of eminent danger and asked him why he's sounding as if he has got everything at the tip of his finger, and under control.

The students continued to grope in the dark of the night in the forest, but thought it wise to take cover in the exact spot they hid themselves from the snake the previous night in case the monster comes back.

As the professor tried to sleep but he couldn't, he then stood up and opened his luggage to get a map of the area, but just as he was rummaging through his bag he stopped suddenly, and sat on the bare floor as his hunch tells him he's in for trouble. That night, the distraught professor couldn't sleep as he stayed awake all night swimming in the imagination of what fate may have befallen his students in the forest, while also being rattled by the failure of Collins and Mallon to bring him help.

At about 10pm, while the students were still maintaining their cover, suddenly the forest became calm, the birds had stopped singing, the wind stopped blowing, the trees stopped whistling and even the frogs stopped croaking. The forest stood still once again, like the night before.

"Shush, the forest has suddenly become calm," said Joel.

"How do you mean?" asked Kelvin.

"Didn't you notice a sudden and extreme quietness in this forest?" asked Kimberly. The students stopped speaking, stayed calm and remain motionless as they listened with keen interest to the unfolding drama in the forest.

"I noticed it, Kelvin," said Amanda.

"Guys, I suppose that monster is on its way. Let's maintain our cover," said Joel.

"Oh my God, not again. Please hold me tight, Kelvin," said Amanda.

A few minutes later, the rustling sound like a moving train emerged from the river and ran through the forest. After a moment, the students could see that same shining object and the same large snake of the previous night, and from a distance they watched the snake leave as it entered the forest.

"Quiet, guys the snake is back," Joel retorted. They began speaking in whispers even as they maintained their cover.

"Let's all stay calm here, at least the snake didn't get to this point last night," said Kelvin.

Amanda was just sobbing uncontrollably in her usual fashion, as she clings tightly onto Kelvin.

"Oh my God, what's happening?" cried Amanda.

"Hey Amanda, shush, stop crying, we're not dead yet," whispered Kelvin.

"Please, let's stop talking and be calm so we don't attract the wrath of this snake," said Kimberly.

"Lee, Lee," said Terry.

"Yeah Terry, what?" asked Lee.

"What about getting the diamond?" said Terry. As luck would have it, Terry is the kind of man who doesn't start a fight but helps to finish it, and a fight with this snake isn't an exception.

"I'm still up for that," said Lee. There was an immediate and intense backlash against Lee, and woe betide Lee if his colleagues perceive he's inviting death on them, and there isn't any room for Lee to justify his move.

Lee, I'm incensed by your obsession with this snake," said Kimberly.

"Lee, I forbid you from putting us in further danger," said Kelvin.

"Let's just keep praying and be hopeful, God's help is the only way out of this," said Joel.

"You've been praying since yesterday and we still remain lost in the forest," said Terry. There isn't a mood for any prayer here, and as Lee joked in his folly, "who do they pray to, the snake or to God?" They all relied on their common sense, yet there isn't popular support for this heist and there's no letting off.

"I didn't come into this forest to assist you in thievery," said Kelvin.

"I'm not thieving anything, and this is nature at its best blessing us with its gift," Lee replied.

"Ok, I suppose when things go south you'll realise this isn't providence but a pure act of thievery," said Joel. Lee remained unfazed by his course-mates' worries, and their starkly different perception of the danger posed by Ngala-na meant Lee's mind is made up to engage this monster in a circus show.

"When the snake is settled, we'll go for the diamond," said Lee.

"Lee, don't do this, please don't blow our cover," Joel pleads.

"I'll not put you in danger. If there's any danger, it'll be me and me alone that'll be in it," Lee promised.

"The military skills you learnt from your dad won't be of any help to you here, this is a mighty snake," said Kimberly.

"Why do you like living on the edge, Lee?" asked Joel. Unfortunately for the students, all effort to dissuade Lee fell on deaf ears as he's hell bent on contesting the diamond with the snake and taking what belongs to the forest.

"Lee, this isn't honey bees, are you sure you can pull this? Because once you blow your cover, you've only got two choices, sink or swim," said Terry.

"Of course, I can," said Lee.

"Lee, this isn't a theatrical slideshow, this is real danger and if you go in there, you'll be dead in minutes. I mean, really, really dead," said Kelvin.

"Please guys, when I smoke the area, just stay calm where you're. Use your clothes to cover your nose, I love you guys," said Lee.

"Just don't do this Lee, this isn't just a large snake, that thing is an embodiment of evil," Joel warned. Since backlash didn't work, some resorted to fear mongering as they tried to make Lee understand that total absence of fear is foolishness, yet all fell on deaf ears. Lee stood in the mist of his friends, and with a disposition of empathy, in a softly spoken manner wished his friends well.

"Wish me luck, but if I don't return, tell my daddy I'm only trying to 'be a man' as he has always encouraged me," said Lee.

"If the need arises, I'll come and join you, brother. We're in this together," Terry promised. "Don't worry, brother; this is the best moment of my life," said Lee.

Lee shook hands with Terry in a manner that signifies brotherhood and left his course-mates and moved about fifty meters closer to the diamond, and without out flinching he blew his cover. He's now at a point of no return and will have to either give in or swim this muddied water to come out from the other end alive. He drew closer, and closer, and then threw two canisters of smoke, throwing one close to the diamond and the other on the very spot the snake was hiding. The snake leaped forward and high above the ground about twenty-five meters from where it was, throwing its massive weight on Lee, who managed to dodge the snake as she landed on the ground. Lee could not use the Taser because the length of the snake and its might was just too massive and beyond Lee's expectation, as the snake swept that entire area of the forest with its body, sweeping Lee off the ground several times. However, the snake could not see clearly because of the smoke, and while the snake was still in her confused state, tearing that entire region of the forest apart, Lee threw his shirt on the diamond and wrapped it immediately denying the snake the opportunity of quickly swallowing the jewel.

Terry, on his part, couldn't bear the rumble in the forest which could be heard in the village of Humaita that's some kilometres away. He became worried about Lee's safety and decided to blow his own cover to give Lee whatever help he might need.

"I think I'll go in there to give Lee whatever help he might need," said Terry.

"The entire forest has been smoked, how then would you know what you're walking into?" asked Joel. Terry is now bound to honour the fraternal pact he had with Lee, even as his colleagues are trying to hold him back, the urge to go into the smoked forest seem stronger.

"I encouraged Lee into doing this, now it's time for me to go in there and help my fellow comrade," said Terry.

"That beast has decimated the forest, and how're you sure Lee is still alive?" asked Amanda. "There's nothing I can do now but to go in there, and if I don't make it, please tell my dad I died trying to save a friend," said Terry. The rumbling in the forest was so intense that Lee's colleagues concluded he's dead because there's no way he's making it out alive.

"Terry, what are you talking about? We cannot afford to lose two friends in one night," said Kelvin.

"Terry, please don't do this," Amanda pleads as she held Terry's hand trying to make him understand. There's now plenty to worry about, and getting cold feet is the least of Terry's worries.

"Only cowards die a thousand times before they are dead," said Terry.

"Are you calling us cowards or what?" asked Kelvin. Kimberly was so frightened, and suddenly, she's literally bursting for a pee and needed to pee immediately, so she excused herself and walked some meters away from the pack to pee. Unfortunately, the fear of Ngala-na meant Kimberly can't stray too far from her friends to have as much privacy as she would normally need for a pee. Terry remained committed to his brotherhood pact with Lee, and he's dead serious with his intention to go into the rumble to find his friend.

"Of course not, I'll be the coward, because I will die a thousand times waiting to see the outcome of Lee's action," said Terry.

"Terry, Terry stop. Don't do this, please," said Amanda as she pleads one last time.

"See you guys, and if I don't make it, I wish you well, my friends," said Terry. The shock of this unfolding drama seems to take its toll on Amanda who couldn't bear to lose another colleague to this forests' beast, yet remain helpless as Lee and Terry were hell bent on having their way.

Terry rushed into the scene of the drama and was immediately swept along with nearby trees. He landed on the ground along with falling trees, though while on the ground, he saw Lee playing dead some distance away. Obviously, Lee had suffered injuries on his shoulder and was immobilised as he could barely walk. Terry was able to crawl to Lee who just lay on the ground playing dead while Ngala-na continued to sweep anything standing.

"Lee, Lee are you ok?" asked Terry. "Yeah I'm fine, but this encounter is worse than I expected, and I can't move," said Lee. "Why, are you hurt?" asked Terry.

"Yeah, my bones are broken, my shoulders seem badly hurt, please help me stand up," said Lee. "Ok, come on," said Terry. Lee was surprised at how Terry found him in the dark of the night. No one would want to touch this monster with a barge pole, yet Lee needs her diamond at all costs. Terry helped Lee up but realised he's unable to stand on his own two feet because he has suffered more than the mere shoulder injury, so he decided to give him support. The guys are using the branches of fallen trees as cover from Ngala-na to plan their escape.

"Come on, grab that diamond, my shirt is already on it," said Lee.

"What! No, let's forget about the diamond, the snake will chase us," said Terry.

"No, I don't think so, the snake can't locate the diamond that's the reason it's ripping the forest apart," said Lee. Terry grabbed the diamond and was about to start running away with it, but realised Lee is limping and isn't out of the woods yet. "What about you?" asked Terry.

"Just run, I'm right behind you. I'm hurt and can't run," said Lee.

"Shush. Your voice is too loud," Terry whispered.

"Ok, just run, Terry. Run with the diamond," said Lee.

While the forest rumbles on, Tyler became worried about the fate of Lee and Terry, and decided it would be appropriate to go into the smoke and find out what fate had befall them, but the rest of his course mates didn't think it's a wise idea, so they pressed him to stay back. Some of the students on the other hand think there is a spell in the forest that's inviting the students into the battle ground.

"Guys, it's important I find out what has happened to Lee and Terry," said Tyler.

"I suppose you can hear, even if you can't see what's going on around us. You can at least hear the entire forest being ripped apart by that monster," said Joel.

"What if they need help?" asked Tyler. The students seem eager to run into this smoked forest one after the other and Joel is now worried that the forest has cast a spell on them, as his colleagues are being sucked in one after another to their death before their eyes. Joel became apprehensive as Tyler wants to follow suit, and a tide of anxiety kept them on the edge as they wondered what comes next.

"Lee left and didn't come back, Terry went for him and hasn't returned either. What then, do you think is going to happen to you if you go into that smoke?" asked Joel.

Now that Christmas chicken has come home to roost, it now behoves the sane students to convince Tyler whom they think is under the spell of the forest to jettison this move that would be quite ruinous. Funnily, Amanda had to use romance which is her strong point to hold Tyler back.

"Tyler, think about your girlfriend; at least stay alive for her," said Amanda. Unfortunately, the last thing Tyler remembered about the girl he loved was the venom she poured on him, because she finds his charm nauseating and couldn't stomach any of his creepiness. In the current circumstance, Vera can't be a reason for Tyler to stay alive.

"Sadly, I don't have a girlfriend and staying safe over a girlfriend will not be necessary," said Tyler.

"What! You don't have a girlfriend?" asked Amanda.

"Of course, I don't. It's sad to say that the one girl I liked gave me a washing down when I tried to become her friend," said Tyler. Now that the idea of using his girlfriend to help him stay alive has failed, Amanda has no other choice but to plead to Tyler's conscience.

"Ok, but please don't go in there for my sake," said Amanda.

"You've got a fiancé, so why should I stay alive for you? Though, I've heard you guys, let's watch the situation for some time," said Tyler. Kelvin had to correct any erroneous impression created by Amanda's plea to avoid any misconception.

"Tyler, she's just trying to help you stay alive, and it doesn't mean she's into you," Kelvin emphasized.

While in the middle of the rumble, Terry tried to run as fast as he could with the diamond, but he'd no idea that Ngala-na was able to see faded traces of the rays of light coming out from the diamond despite it being wrapped severally with a black T-shirt. Ngala-na didn't hesitate as she dived at the moving diamond, and landed on Terry, then the diamond fell from Terry, but still wrapped in the clothe. Sadly, Ngala-na was busy ripping the forest apart at random without paying particular attention to Lee and Terry, possibly because she couldn't see without the diamond.

Lee rushed to Terry's aid.

"Are you ok?" asked Lee.

"Err, hmm. I don't think so, my knee is dislocated," said Terry. Lee lifted Terry up, to help him escape the wrath of this monster.

"Please, let's be fast about this before we lose our window of opportunity," said Lee.

"What do you mean by window of opportunity?" asked Terry. The density of the smoke is reducing fast, and within a short while the snake might be able to manage this surprise attack better, and that implies death for Lee and Terry.

"The snake can't see clearly yet and it's still confused. The moment she regains herself, we're dead," said Lee.

"Should we abandon the diamond and run for our lives?" asked Terry.

"No, that won't be proper, we're already in this, and it seems the snake can still see the rays of light. That's why it attacked you," said Lee. It took Terry a few seconds to think of a way of escaping this brouhaha with the snake without further ado.

"If that's the case, take off your jeans and give it to me. While holding Lee's Jeans in his hand, Terry also took off his own trousers.

"What do you want to do with them?" asked Lee.

"Just watch me," said Terry. He used his trouser and Lee's jeans to wrap the diamond in a manner that prevented Ngala-na from seeing any ray of light emanating from the diamond.

"Let's leave here now because the smoke will soon fade away," said Lee.

"Unfortunately we both can't run because of our injuries," said Terry. They both limped along, giving each other some support and making a run for it as they held tightly onto their trophy.

"I don't think it's a good idea to run towards our course mates to avoid putting them in danger," said Lee.

"In case the snake is after us? Then that'll be a good idea," said Terry.

"Let's go south," said Lee. They changed direction and limped as fast as their weak and injured legs could carry them despite their injuries, until they were out of range of the mighty snake and hid themselves.

"You made it, Lee. I'm proud of you," said Terry.

"No, we made it, Terry. If not for you, I wouldn't have survived this," said Lee.

"I pushed you into doing this, so I've to support you even when my life is at stake," said Terry.

While all this drama was going on in the forest throughout that night, the village of Humaita stood still since nobody could sleep or wink an eye, because the noise of rumbling and fallen trees could be heard several kilometres away. As Ngala-na swept and tore the forest apart in a mad rage, even the professor and his students were alarmed by the thunderous rumbling, and this increased his confusion and frustration. At this point there was confusion everywhere; firstly for the natives in Humaita, then the professor and his students were the next in this confusion, and finally were the rest of the missing students who remained worried about what may have happened to Lee and Terry.

The restless professor who was already awake rushed to Noaita to inquire what the problem might be.

"My visitor, how're you?" asked Noaita.

"Noaita, I've come to find out what that noise is about," said Prof. Hendrix.

"I don't know what that's about but you can see every villager outside their hut because they're equally afraid," said Noaita. The professor looked around and saw that most of the villagers are awake as most of them stood in front of their huts with their oil lamps well lit.

"You know my students are in that forest. Can you assure me they're alive and safe?" asked Prof. Hendrix.

"I don't know what to say, but tomorrow we'll definitely enter that forest to look for them," Noaita promised. With the nature of the noise coming from the forest, tomorrow seems like a decade away. The professor needed some level of assurance that tomorrow will surely come and his students trapped in the forest will be fine and safe. The soft spoken tone of Noaita, has the calmness to pour cool water on the fire of a hot temper and that doesn't seem to sooth the professor's anxiety, and yet becoming angry at the situation won't help him either.

"The noises coming from that forest just dampen my hope of finding these students alive," said Prof. Hendrix.

"Let's just be calm. Tomorrow you'll get all the help you need," said Noaita.

"Thank you, I'll return to my hut," said Prof. Hendrix.

"Just stay awake, as we all try to understand what's going on in our forest," said Noaita.

The professor returned to his hut and stood by the door, watching what was going on outside. Just as the professor returned and stood by the door Vera rushed to meet him as he stood by the door.

"Professor, what's going on?" asked Vera.

"I don't know, this is an unusual noise. That was why I woke up and stood by the door", said Prof. Hendrix.

"What do we do now?" asked Christian.

"I've just met with Noaita, and he said the villagers don't know what's going on either," said Prof. Hendrix.

"Then this is serious!" exclaimed Beata.

"We'll do nothing; I've been observing the noise to see if the danger is coming in this direction," said Prof. Hendrix. It's blindingly obvious that the professor lacks the virtue of divorcing his feelings from the realities on the ground as the concerns of his students' means he must continue to muddle through until it's all over.

"Professor, what about our course-mates? I hope the noise we're hearing has got nothing to do with them," asked Johnny.

"How do you mean, Johnny?" asked Prof. Hendrix. Johnny was a little dramatic as he couldn't think any better, other than filling his mind with all manner of gibberish as he attempted to give a riveting description of the happenings in the forest.

"Maybe a monster is eating them up, or rather tearing them apart?" said Johnny.

"The noise coming out of that forest reminds me of apocalypse," said Christian.

"Jonny! Why should you think such a thing about your colleagues? We need to be positive, at least for their sake," said Prof. Hendrix.

Unsurprisingly, the professor took exception to Johnny's comment and think such a sordid joke is uncalled for at this moment. Being faint hearted in times like this is expected but it isn't enough to tuck in one's tail between one's legs and run the opposite direction abandoning one's course mates in the forest.

"With this kind of thunderous sound coming from the forest, will we be able to enter the forest tomorrow?" asked Samantha.

"Of course, at least we returned from the same forest about six hours ago, and we were not consumed," said Christian.

"Ok, what do we do now?" asked Johnny.

"Go back to your huts and stay awake while we assess the situation as it unfolds," said Prof. Hendrix. On a second thought the professor asked his students to stay in front of their huts as opposed to staying inside as it will help them to keep a watchful eye on the happenings around them. Without further ado, it now behoves on the professor to extricate his students from this ancient forest, and sadly, the professor isn't agnostic that there's more to this forest than meets the eye, yet he's determined not to exacerbate the panic in his already troubled students.

"Professor, if we notice anything strange, do we call your attention?" asked Vera.

"Yes, of course! You might see me first if the need for an action arises," said Prof. Hendrix. The students left for their various huts, but soon banded together in front of one of the huts where both they and their professor can keep an eye on each other, and remained awe struck as they stayed awake all night.

That same night, while most of the villagers were all outside their huts worrying about what the problem was in the forest. The village head (Ta-Piraha), who was also troubled, sent for the chief priest. Moments later, the Chief walked into the palace with his gigida, he then spread out his skin mat and sat on it as he attempts to make himself comfortable.

"I sent for you, chief priest, because I don't know what's going on," said Ta-Piraha.

"My king, the villagers are worried as well because they've never experienced anything of this sort," said the Chief Priest.

"Since I was born, I don't think I've heard a noise like this coming from our forest," Ta-Piraha retorted.

"My king, the forest is troubled and I can feel it in my spirit," replied the Chief priest.

"What troubles the forest? I want you to do further consultations, please tell me," said Ta-Piraha. The norm has always been that Chief priests don't consult oracles late in the night, and this norm isn't going to change even in the current circumstance.

"Tell you? You know its midnight, and I can't do any consultation tonight," said the Chief Priest. Consulting the gods in the wee hours of the night could put the chief priest on the receiving end of the gods' ire. This ancient quirky tradition must be kept, and the chief priest isn't in a hurry to make a break for it, so as not to get the short end of the stick.

"Do we wait until we're consumed? There are crises around us and you can hear it as well," said Ta-Piraha.

"I'm well aware of the troubles around us, but I can't consult the gods tonight, at least you know the tradition," said the Chief priest. Ta-Piraha's ears aren't clogged, but his caring nature means he can't wait till tomorrow but protests against observing this ancient norm when things are falling apart around them.

"What you're implying is that our gods are asleep, and does it mean if we are in danger the gods will remain asleep until we're all consumed?" Ta-Piraha protested. Without due care and caution thrown into the wind, things could get sour between the village head and the chief priest who are the guardians of this village.

"Please, my king, I'll advise that you mind your utterances to avoid incurring the wrath of the gods," said the Chief Priest.

"Yes, you're right, tomorrow morning we'll consult the gods," said Ta-Piraha.

The slight disagreement between the village head and the chief priest is a sign of the fraught atmosphere precipitated by this kerfuffle. The debate over whether to consult the gods while it's still dark suddenly reached a boiling point.

The Village head and the Chief priest suddenly realised there isn't any need to divide and conquer to appease whatever is behind the troubles in their forest. This chief priest is pathologically stone-faced, and laughter isn't something she does voluntarily, he'd to practice how to laugh, but that does not necessarily mean he's a bad man as far as his village is concerned.

Immediately after the chief priest left the palace, the worried village head remained restless as tomorrow seem a decade away, so he sent his guards to summon the head hunter immediately.

"My king, you sent for me," said Anteym.

"Yes, I sent for you. Did you hear the noise coming from the forest?" asked Ta-Piraha.

"Yes, my king, my family and I have been awake for some hours," said Anteym. The noise coming from the forest is general knowledge but the reason behind the noise remains a mystery to all the villagers except for the students currently in the forest.

"Do you know what that's about? Because I don't," asked Ta-Piraha.

"I'm a hunter who knows the forest very well but I must confess I've no Idea of what this is about," Anteym replied.

"This is the last day of the sun, but we've never experienced any of this in the past years," said Ta-Piraha. Apart from being terrified, the noise alone from this forest is waging a psychological war on the villagers but understanding the hoo-ha behind the noise remains a mystery for all and sundry.

"I've observed the days of the sun from my childhood but nothing like this was ever experienced," said Anteym.

"Please gather other hunters and be at alert, we'll need to protect our village if necessary," said Ta-Piraha.

"Ok my king, let me do that right away," replied Anteym. On a second thought, just as Anteym turned to leave, the village head beckons on Anteym. "Wait, Anteym, some of my guards will join you to help out as well," said Ta-Piraha.

"Ok, thank you, my king," said Anteym. He turned and left the palace and waited for the king's guard outside.

However, the other five out of the missing seven are worried about what has happened to Lee and Terry as they witness the forest being ripped apart by Ngala-na.

"This snake is sweeping this forest clean and tearing down all the trees around," said Tyler.

"I'm suggesting we move backward because this destruction is getting closer to us," said Kelvin. They then moved some distance backward, farther away from the destruction before them, yet they remained scared stiff, while Ngala-na wreaks havoc. After waiting for about two hours, without any sign of Lee and Terry, the worry for their safety increased.

"Why haven't Lee and Terry returned?" said Tyler.

"Who knows what may have happened, they're supposed to be back by now," said Kelvin.

"Who do you think will walk into that destruction you just witnessed and come out unhurt?" asked Amanda.

The persistent infighting among these students abated as they seem to comfort themselves over the loss of Lee and Terry who walked into a death trap and never made it back. Thanks to Lee and Terry, Tyler was able to belatedly understand the risk of walking into that smoke to search for his friends. Kimberly then turned to Tyler.

"Is that what you would've walked into?" she asked.

"I'm surprised at the strength of this snake," said Tyler.

Worried sick that his friends are already in the belly of the beast that isn't just a snake but an evil monster, Tyler suddenly became thankful to his friends who constrained him from going into the smoked forest in search of Lee and Terry.

Yet, Kimberly didn't hesitate to remind his friends of how Lee's foolishness could've resulted in a catastrophic consequence that led Terry to a fatal end, and it's hard to grasp why Terry took this big jump into the unknown, and their worries have quadrupled to quite a depressing level. Their conversation suddenly became a scattergun as they shifted their conversation from how evil the snake itself is to the size of the snake, and describing it as bigger than the biggest anaconda on the face of the earth.

"Why should you be surprised, don't you watch discovery channels? This snake is far bigger than the ones you see on the Discovery Channel," said Kelvin.

"Thank you guys for stopping me from going in there, but I still felt my going into that smoke would've saved them," said Tyler.

After about four hours of struggling to save her diamond, Nga-la-na left the forest completely torn apart, and there was a sigh of relief as Ngala-na finally made the same rustling sound like a fast moving train as she went back into the River Maici at about 3am.

"It's like the snake has gone back to the river," said Terry.

"That's good, which means we conquered the snake," Lee said ecstatically.

"Let's join our course mates now that the danger is over," said Terry. This monster's blood still boils, but it has returned to the river and it's now safe to grope in the dark. After all, when the cat is out of town, the mice are free to roam.

"But it's still dark, and some wild animals could be roaming the forest, so it's advisable to remain in one spot when it's dark," said Lee.

"They might get into much more danger trying to locate us if we don't get to them first," said Terry. Ngala-na's return to river Maici gave the all-clear signal for Lee and Terry to come out of cover and join their terrified course mates who thought they didn't make it alive. The forest remains dark as dawn is still a few hours away, but now that the landmarks has been decimated by Ngala-na, some form of lighting will be needed to help them locate their course mates. They then hurtled through the dark of the forest, yet they funnily couldn't tell what direction their friends are. "That's a wise thought, and glad your phone is still alive?" said Terry. "Ok that's good, let's join the others," said Lee. As they proceed to join their course mates, Terry checked for his phone and couldn't find it. "Lee, I can't find my phone," said Terry.

"You may have lost it during our encounter with the snake, we'll look for it later in the day," said Lee.

They continued and Lee switched on his phone as they proceeded but funnily Lee's phone is almost out of power and could barely do the job. "My phone is already beeping, let's see if we can make do with this," said Lee. "Yeah, it's beeping because it's about to go off. Let's just be quick, and it'll help us locate them," said Terry.

Fifteen minutes later, after too many twists and turns, the wait for news about Lee and Terry is now about to come to an end as the two students assumed to have been dead have returned alive, and with a trophy in hand.

"Guys, can you see that faded light coming towards us?" asked Tyler, who has been watching out for any sign of life out there in the forest.

"You're right, let's just watch because it could be light from the eyes of an animal," said Kelvin.

"That can't be light from an animal's eye. That must either be Terry or Lee looking for us," said Tyler. The anxiety increased as the light drew closer, even though the best bet will be that the light is Lee and Terry returning to the pack, yet it could be a wild beast strolling past them.

"Let's not put ourselves in danger, and its better we wait a little while," said Joel. Tyler rushed out from his hiding place and screamed. "Lee, is that you?" said Tyler. "Not just Lee, it's both of us," said Terry.

The students were enraptured as they couldn't hold their excitement because their friends thought to be dead are now back. Tyler and Kelvin rushed to embrace them. "Oh, I'm happy you guys are alive," said Tyler.

"Ouch, easy guys, my shoulder is injured," said Lee.

"What's that you're holding?" asked Joel. "The diamond, of course," said Lee. Surprised that the diamond is now in their grasp Kelvin ecstatically tried to touch the wrapped item.

"What, you mean the diamond? You guys must be from the warrior clan," said Kelvin.

"You guys are something else; I never knew you were this courageous," said Kimberly. Amanda enthusiastically grabbed the item and tried unwrapping it to take a peek at the content, but Lee seems to prefer it's best to keep the jewel hidden from its forest.

"Unwrap it, let's see!" exclaimed Amanda.

"No, not now," said Lee.

"Why not now? I want to see it," Amanda insists.

"If this diamond is unwrapped it'll give light to the snake and that'll be deadly," said Terry. After Lee stopped Amanda from unwrapping the diamond, Terry's explanation of why it isn't wise to unwrap the diamond while they remain in the forest made sense and they stopped pestering to take a peek at the wrapped item. The seven missing are now back together in one piece, the pack is now complete. "When it's day, we'll unwrap it, but is still dark and the snake will locate us if we do that now," said Lee.

CHAPTER

FIVE

3rd of June – Third Day in Humaita

The next morning, Ta-Piraha sent for the chief priest to find out what went wrong in the forest the night before.

"I sent for you, because I'm still worried about last night," said Ta-Piraha.

"Let me consult our gods," said the Chief Priest.

"Please consult them and let me know what went wrong," said Ta-Piraha.

The chief spread out his animal skin mat on the floor and infusing some of his usual semantic in his incantations as he consults his oracle to hear from the gods.

"The forest was desecrated," said the Chief Priest.

"How do you mean the forest was desecrated, who desecrated the forest?" asked Ta-Piraha curiously.

"The students we are looking for are responsible," said the Chief priest. Ta-Piraha adjusted his seat following this new revelation as he listened keenly to the Chief priest. It's obvious that this chief priest isn't out to jump-scare the village head, but for all it's worth, this matter is fast turning into a carbuncle that requires delicate handling by all and sundry.

"But those students can't make the kind of noise we heard yesterday," said Ta-Piraha.

"It was Ngala-na that made that noise, because she was angry," said the Chief Priest. Surprised at what could have angered Ngala-na to the point of exhibiting its fury in this manner became a matter of great concern to Ta-Piraha who decided to query the oracle further.

"What did they do to her that angered her this much?" asked Ta-Piraha.

"They took something that belonged to her," said the Chief Priest.

"What did they take and how do we go about this?" asked Ta-Piraha. The action of the needling students is now brought to the fore, and now, this sticky situation requires urgent attention to prevent a reoccurrence of yesterday's experience.

"Let's wait for the students to come but I see more destruction," said the Chief Priest.

"You said destruction, let's wait for the students to come," said Ta-Piraha. The village head then inquired about other concerns as he asked the chief priest if the hunters will return safely if they go in search of the students. Unsurprisingly, the village head had to prioritise concerns by putting things into perspective. Firstly, the safety of his guests, and the next will be about addressing why Ngala-na was wrathful.

"Yes they'll be safe, and the hunters will find the students," said the Chief Priest.

"Ok chief priest, you can go. I'll get back to you," said Ta-Piraha.

After getting a positive confirmation that his hunters will return safely if they enter the forest, Ta-Piraha gave the professor twenty hunters to assist him in searching for his students. Noaita tried to assuage the professor's fear as the search party entered into the forest.

"My visitors, don't worry, we've been assured the forest is safe despite the noise we heard last night," said Noaita. The professor was surprised to see the hunters split themselves into two groups as they go into the forest.

"Noaita, what are they doing?" asked Prof. Hendrix.

"They're sharing themselves into two groups to enable them cover the entire forest," said Noaita. Professor Hendrix couldn't afford any hesitation in the search for his students as he wants his students whisked out of the forest immediately.

"But aren't they too slow?" the professor retorted.

"Professor, don't worry, the students are safe," said Noaita.

"How do you know this? Because last night you couldn't assure me of their safety," the professor protested.

"The chief priest said so," said Noaita.

"And you believe everything he says?" asked Prof. Hendrix curiously.

"Yes, because he has never been wrong," said Noaita.

"Then did he tell you whether we'll find my students?" asked Prof. Hendrix.

"Yes, he said we'll find them," Noaita assured the professor. While this conversation between Noaita and the professor persists, Johnny stood still for a while with his focus fixed on Anteym, the head hunter who seemed busy giving directives to his fellow hunters on the direction of the search.

"Oh, look at that hunter," said Johnny.

"What about him?" Christian interjected.

"That's the head hunter, and I like his frame," said Beata.

"He's huge but I hate his imposing stature," said Johnny.

"Are you jealous of him because of your small frame?" asked Beata. Johnny is small-statured but a highly irritable person and sometimes feisty. Funnily, Beata showed no hesitation to take him on as she steered the conversation away from the head hunter to banter with Johnny.

"Stop acting naive," Johnny protested as Beata steered the conversation away from looks to emotion.

"The hunter you're talking about is the head hunter in this village," said Noaita.

"You guys should keep screaming out their names and continue to look for trails," said Prof. Hendrix. After the professor intervened to stop the ensuing kerfuffle between Beata and Johnny, Beata kept screaming out loud the names of her course mates.

"Amanda, Kimberly, Tyler, can you hear me?" asked Beata.

"The task of trying to locate these students in the forest is arduous," said Prof. Hendrix.

"Don't worry, you'll find them," Noaita assured the professor. The professor encouraged his students to scream louder while the search continues.

"Please scream louder," said Prof. Hendrix.

"Please, let's keep walking fast to remain in the company of the hunters," advised Noaita.

As they entered deeper into the forest, they got to the point where the destruction of the previous night took place; even the hunters were shocked and surprised at what may have happened.

"What the hell! What happened here?" asked Johnny.

The professor and his students, including Noaita, were all taken aback by the level of destruction in the wake of the previous night's rumble in the forest. The professor couldn't hold back his emotion as the shock of the aftermath of last night's horror was laid bare.

"But we passed here yesterday, didn't we?" asked Prof. Hendrix.

"I've never seen a thing like this all my life," said Noaita.

"This looks like a place where multiple bomb blasts took place," said Christian.

The professor and his students stood statute still for a while drowned in thought of what might have been responsible for this brutal blow to this forest.

"Do you mean our course-mates were in this forest when this happened?" asked Johnny.

"What actually happened here?" asked Samantha. The sight of the destruction got to Vera and she began to sob because it dampened her hope of seeing Tyler again.

"I hope these guys are safe. How can a person be alive around such destruction!" exclaimed Vera.

From the other end, the missing seven heard the call from the professor's end.

"Listen guys, I heard a voice calling out to us," said Lee. They became calm and listened keenly to hear if someone is calling out for them. "I heard Tyler's name and I can hear Kimberly's; that's Vera's voice, I suppose," said Joel.

"You mean Vera is screaming my name?" asked Tyler, as he expressed his surprise.

"Yes, what's it about?" said Kimberly.

"Then, I've just got a reason to stay alive," said Tyler.

"Let's start screaming louder, so they can hear us and come to our direction," said Lee.

The seven students began to scream as loud as they could until they stretched their vocal cords to the limits.

"Mallon, Johnny, Vera!" screamed Tyler. This time the voice of the missing seven reached the professor and his entourage and John screamed out loud in return.

"They can hear us," said Lee.

They began to run towards the professor and his search party. Twenty minutes later the missing seven were reunited with the professor and their course mates. It was quite a very emotional moment for both the professor and his students as most of the students shed tears of joy; even the professor could not hide his excitement.

The hunters in the company of the professor and his students sent signals through sounds to the other group of hunters, to let them know the students in question had been found.

"Professor, I'm happy your students are safe," said Noaita. After allowing the professor and his students a few minutes to celebrate their reunion, the head hunter drew closer to Noaita and gave him a message from Ta-Piraha.

"Noaita, Ta-Piraha will want to see these students in his palace," said Anteym.

"Ok, they'll come to the palace later in the day to see him," replied Noaita. Running off to the palace to answer to the village head's call might seem premature when the professor and his student haven't put the record straight.

"I told you not to go into the forest without a guide," said Prof. Hendrix.

"But Professor, we told you before we left," said Amanda.

"You told me you wanted to walk around the village and that didn't include walking into the deep end of the Amazon, and your walk into the Amazon has caused us so much trouble," said Prof. Hendrix. While the reunion was going on, attention suddenly turned to Vera whose excitement was beyond explanation as she just kept hugging Tyler continuously.

"Good to see you," said Vera. Tyler was taken aback by Vera's sudden disposition towards him and remained mortified.

"Vera, I'm lost. What happened to your prejudice and paranoia towards me?" asked Tyler. The highly impassioned Vera didn't hesitate to tell of her change of heart.

""I suddenly realised that those tiny little gestures like your smiles, winking of eyes, the unwanted attention, and even interjecting in my conversation in a manner that gets me kicking off, means a lot to me. They make me feel special," said Vera. Tyler soon realised he has a hold on Vera, as she confessed to Tyler that she takes no delight in vexing him, but urged him to forget the awkwardness of the past because she now sees a future that involves two of them together.

"Terry, why are you limping? And you, Lee, what happened to your posture? You seem to be bent," said Prof. Hendrix.

"We had some form of accident," said Lee. "What kind of accident?" asked Prof. Hendrix.

The professor and the rest of the students with him are keen to know how these two students suffered their injuries, even though their hunch tells them that Lee and Terry were victims of the destruction of the previous night. Funnily, Terry was quick to interject and said they collided with each other while trying to find their way in the dark.

"Then you'll need medical attention, maybe first aid will do," said Prof. Hendrix. But it's blindingly obvious that Terry's story is short of truth because it's just only him and Lee that were scantily dressed in their underpants. Mere collision between two people shouldn't resort to taking off one's trousers.

"Terry, why're you and Lee wearing just your underpants, and why aren't you wearing your trousers?" asked Beata.

"They used it to wrap a diamond," Amanda whispered.

"I'm not following, and where did the diamond come from?" asked Johnny. Now that the gini is out of the bottle, Lee felt it's proper to limit the news of this diamond within their camp.

"That's ok guys; we'll talk about that when we get to our camp," said Lee.

"Collins and Mallon aren't here, where are they?" asked Kelvin.

"They went to Manicore to get us help," said Vera. Collins is another vocal student who's truly missed by Tyler, but the joy of having Vera suddenly falling heads over heels for him compensated Collins's absence.

"What sort of help are you talking about?" asked Tyler.

"They went to inform the university authority of your sudden disappearance in the forest, to see if they could send us help in finding you guys," said Beata.

"Professor, sorry for all the trouble we've put you through," said Joel. The passive apology seems not enough to pacify the ailed professor who has saved those tough talks for later.

"We'll talk about the troubles you've caused us when we get to the camp," said Prof. Hendrix.

"Guys, do you've any idea of what's responsible for the destruction we saw in that forest?" asked Johnny. Rattled by the destruction that was left behind from last night, the students are now in a quest for answers as to what might be responsible for this level of damage to the forest. For all it's worth, these students don't need to look any further in their quest for answers as to what's behind the destruction to the forest because they're asking their colleagues who witnessed the destruction first hand.

"We saw it with our eyes, Professor. It's a snake," said Kimberly.

"What, a snake! What sort of snake could cause such destruction?" asked Prof. Hendrix.

"Then you guys are lucky to be alive," said Christian.

"This is no ordinary snake, it's a monster with a satanic aura, and it's a fourteen-meter-long snake," said Kelvin. The description of this snake seems over embellished but the destruction the snake left behind didn't seem to overestimate size of the snake either. The description of the snake as some kind of heavy-weight anaconda that weighs hundreds of tons seem fitting for the destruction left in its wake, but in all sincerity even science have no record of such mighty snake and this left the professor quite puzzled.

"The longest snake on record is less than ten meters long, did you take measurement of this snake to know it's fourteen meters long?" asked Prof. Hendrix.

"Professor, the destruction you saw speaks for itself," said Tyler.

"I suppose so, but you sound more like a sensationalist?" said Prof. Hendrix. The professor had no idea that his students had a close encounter with the monster that wrecked the destruction of the previous night.

"I usually assist my dad in taking measurements and I can give you a fairly accurate measurement from a distance," said Lee.

"You're all looking pale and you'll need to eat something, but a good rest when we get to the village might be helpful," said Prof. Hendrix.

They're all glad that the drama and uncertainty is over, and Kimberly can't wait to return to normal life but it's only a matter of time that she would know if that'll happen or not.

"Err, I can't wait to get to the village, but I'm so happy to be home and alive," said Kimberly. The students continued chatting among themselves and catching up as they walk to the village. Moments later, they returned to the village and the professor turned to Noaita.

"Thank you very much, my friend. You've been a good friend," said Prof. Hendrix.

"Professor, the village head will like to see these students later," said Noaita.

"Which of the students, and what for?" asked Prof. Hendrix.

"The ones we just found in the forest, but I don't know why he wants to see them," said Noaita. Asking the student to report immediately at the place might be too much to ask from the professor at this point, particularly now that the students are famished and looking poorly kept after spending days wandering in the forest.

"Ok, they'll come over but they'll have to eat and rest, and as you can see they're already looking pale.

"You should also thank Anteym, the head hunter, for using his fellow hunters for this search," said Prof. Hendrix.

Moments after the professor and his students arrived in the village, Noaita went his way and the professor and his students went into their huts. But before they went into their various huts the professor decided to address their injuries.

"Lee, you and Terry need medical attention," said Prof. Hendrix.

"Professor, I'll be fine, I just need to get some rest," said Lee.

"I don't think you'll be just fine by rest alone with the way you look," said Prof. Hendrix. Terry on his part felt that making light of his injuries will get the professor off his back for now until they fully disclose the source of their injuries.

"I just need some hot balm tended on my knee and I believe I'll be fine as well," said Terry. Since these guys are locking up and aren't giving out much, the professor then turned to Joel whom he seems to take a liking to of late.

"Joel, tell me what happened in that forest. How did you guys manage to escape the wrath of that snake?" asked Prof. Hendrix.

"We were in the dark and heard a rustling sound and minutes later we saw a shining object, a diamond to be precise, then saw this mighty snake," said Joel. Johnny cuts into the conversation and laid it all bare before the professor.

"Professor, they stole the diamond belonging to the snake," said Johnny.

"What diamond are you talking about?" the professor asked curiously. The professor looked lost and dumbfounded as the conversation unfolds the horror and adventure of his supposed innocent student.

"That's it, with Terry," said Johnny.

"Have you seen it?" the professor queried further.

"No, I haven't, but that's it wrapped in there," said Johnny.

"Is it true?" asked Prof. Hendrix.

"Yes Professor," Johnny replied. "Let me see it," said Prof. Hendrix. The professor was curious to verify the students' assertion that their misfortunes resulted in a trophy. Terry quickly unwrapped the diamond and handed it to the professor who's eager to corroborate the narrative of his students.

"Guys, this is pure diamond," said Johnny. The students were open-mouthed as they all gathered around the diamond. Even Lee that stole the diamond hasn't had the opportunity to take a closer look at his trophy before now. They held their trophy and celebrated their victory over Ngala-na, with shouts and cheers.

"How did this diamond come about?" the professor asked further.

"The diamond is from the snake, she vomited it," said Joel. The professor himself was lost for words, as he remained speechless for a while, and when he eventually opened his mouth.

"I've heard about snakes vomiting diamonds but I thought it was just a myth," said Prof. Hendrix.

"Yes Professor, I used to think that way but was awestricken when I witnessed this first hand," said Joel.

"How did you collect the diamond from the snake? asked Prof. Hendrix. The professor is keen to know because it's quite impossible for the snake to hand its diamond willingly to these students. So far, the students' narrative about how this diamond came about is lacking the fine details.

"Lee and I fought the snake and then we took the diamond and ran away," said Terry.

Terry's response wasn't satisfactory enough for the professor who tried to juxtapose the aftermath of the destruction of the previous night and the ability of these two students to overpower such a snake.

"I said how? Because I know the two of you can't fight with the snake that caused the destruction we saw in that forest," said Prof. Hendrix.

"I threw military grade smoke canisters at the snake, she became confused, then I went for the diamond," said Lee. The professor is now beginning to piece the puzzle together as more information come to light.

"I guess the snake was responsible for the injuries both of you sustained?" asked Prof. Hendrix.

"Yes Professor," said Lee. "I suppose this is some form of heist, and do you know you would've gotten yourself killed?" the professor stressed.

"I'm sorry, Professor. I underestimated the risk and in truth the snake was actually powerful," said Lee.

"Do you know your actions could've endangered your course-mates?" asked Prof. Hendrix.

"We actually misjudged the strength of the snake and it was quite risible," Terry confessed.

Time for jokes and messing about is over, it's now time for telling off, because Professor Hendrix is now talking tough, and it now dawned on the students that their professor isn't a fan of dare devils that do things on a whim.

"That aside, what were you guys doing seven kilometres into the forest without a guide?" asked Prof. Hendrix.

"We were just having a walk in the forest when we spotted that bloodlike rock, and decided to get closer to the rock," said Kelvin. Sadly, awfulising or minimising their worrisome forest experience won't make their idiocy any less.

"I specifically said we'll go into the forest with a guide," said Prof. Hendrix.

"Professor, you told us, we're sorry; the strange thing is that we suddenly lost our way the moment we left that rock," said Joel.

Meanwhile, just as the professor and his students celebrate their reunion with cheers, Collins and Mallon remained locked up in a cell in the village of Parana for the second day. Kamti didn't hesitate to pay a visit to the prisoners after his return from his farm on their second day in captivity.

"My friends, how are you?" Asked Kamti.

"Kamti, we're tired and hungry and couldn't sleep, what else do you expect?" asked Collins.

"I'll go and speak to our village head, to see if he can let you go," Kamti promised. Kamti's emotion is now torn between being nice to these innocent young men and his loyalty to his people, sadly the later takes priority.

"You know we don't deserve this?" said Mallon.

"I understand, just that you're suffering as a result of the action of some of your people," said Kamti.

"Speak to him, and please, just do your best," Collins pleads. Kamti left Mallon and Collins and went for an intercessory mission, not minding that such mission could mean he's turning the barrel on himself and shooting himself in the foot. Unsurprisingly, Mallon didn't hesitate to expresse his disappointment at his professor immediately Kamti left.

"Why hasn't Professor Hendrix come for us, and why did he abandon us here?" Mallon asked in a quite distressing tone.

"I don't think he knows we're in this quagmire," said Collins.

"This whole research thing looks like an entrapment," said Mallon.

"I don't think so, Mallon. It's just hard luck," replied Collins. Mallon's sober reflection of the too many strokes of ill luck that befell them since the beginning of this research isn't just a knee-jerk reaction, but the failures of this expedition got to him as he became overwhelmed and got taken over by pettiness.

"Then why are these entanglements coming up? Maybe the professor knew something we didn't," said Mallon.

"Don't talk like that, the professor never asked Kelvin and the other students to go into the forest, they went on their own volition and he also found himself running around trying to sort out this mess," said Collins.

"Then what are our chances of leaving this cell? What if the village head says no?" asked Mallon. Mallon has now lost faith in the professor and even in himself, and he's beginning to give in to despair as he now fears he will die in this village. It now behoves on Collins to help Mallon stay strong and be hopeful because all hope isn't lost.

"Just be strong, the professor will come for us, we just have to be strong," said Collins.

"Stop trying to assuage my fears," Mallon retorted. "I'm not trying to attenuate your fears; I'm only asking you to stay strong," said Collins.

Kamti meets with his village head to see if he can secure the release of Collins and Mallon but this visit puts Kamti in a tricky position.

"Kamti, what brought you here this early?" asked the village head.

"My king, please, I came with respect to those white men in the cell," said Kamti.

"What about them? Aren't you supposed to be in the farm?" asked the village head.

"Since they aren't the actual people that stole your bronze head, I want to crave your indulgence for their release," said Kamti. It's possible to eat a sour fruit and a different and neutral person feels the sensitivity of the sourness on his teeth, this is now the fate of Collins and Mallon. Unfortunately, this is outside the purview of Karma.

"They're all of the same species, and I don't want them to steal more things from this village," said the village head.

"I don't think they have the tendency to steal, because they're just passing and heading to Manicore," said Kamti. The move to advocate rather than intercede for these two prisoners seems to rattle the village head's cage and this could precipitate opening a can of worms, and sadly, Kamti might find himself scampering for safety when the worms starts sprawling all over the place.

"How do you know? Is it because you were not incriminated over the loss of our bronze head?" asked the village head.

"Oh, my King? You know I've no hand in that," said Kamti.

"You remember you were their interpreter, you were the closest to them, and I just decided to overlook your role in that theft," said the village head.

"But you know my hands are clean, even the chief priest confirmed my innocence," Kamti pleads. With accusations flying here and there, Kamti decided to tread carefully to avoid being sucked in as there isn't a need for him to dip his feathers in this flutter.

"Go to your farm and pursue your business, and I'll release them on my own terms," said the village head.

"Ok, thank you my lord. I have to get going," said Kamti. Kamti tucked his tail between his legs and ran off, as things almost went south for him. His effort to plead for Collins and Mallon has failed woefully, and he wouldn't risk being perceived by his village head as a pot stirrer who deserves being put in his place. Unsurprisingly, as Kamti realised he has no dog in this fight that's about to chafe him under, he decided to make a run for it, but the village head called him back.

"Kamti, make sure they eat well. Come to the palace and get food for them," said the village head.

"My king, they're refusing to eat their food," said Kamti.

"Try to encourage them to eat but I'll release them on my own terms," said the village head.

"Ok my king, thank you," said Kamti. For all it's worth, Kamti is obviously a man who has no single bone for rebellion in his body. He's known to do as told, and even if asked to go to the moon, he will never question the rationale behind the assignment, provided he's given a ladder to help him reach the moon.

Instead of running off, Kamti had a change of mind and decided to make one last visit to Mallon and Collins, whose ears are itching for good news from the village head. The moment Kamti walked in, Mallon was quick to ask for feedback because he couldn't stay another minute in this God forsaken cell.

"Kamti, how did it go?" asked Mallon.

"My friends, I'm sorry, the village head wishes to keep you here until he is sure of your mission," said Kamti.

"Why didn't you tell him we're researchers?" Mallon protested.

"Those behind your predicament were researchers as well," replied Kamti. It's now embarrassingly obvious that this village head is keen on clipping the wings of these foreigners by keeping them under lock and key before they leave him blindsided and rob him of another precious jewel.

"Tell him we're only passing to Manicore, we're stationed in Humaita," said Collins.

"What were you doing in the village of Humaita?" asked Kamti. Though, Kamti was bloody sick of the pains inflicted on these guys, but giving his village head the run around by going behind his back to make contact with Humaita on behalf of these prisoners might mean his head would end up on the Plata.

"We're doing research in their forest and there are fifteen of us, plus one, sixteen," said Collins.

"You should have told me about this," said Kamti.

"If your village head is determined not to let us go, then no matter what you say, he wouldn't let us go," said Collins. Rather amusingly, it's now obvious to Collins that the village head is bent on keeping them behind bars irrespective of whatever their defence is. Arguably, the short end of the stick has now been reserved for Mallon and Collins and they just have to accept their fate.

"Then what can we do about this, Collins?" asked Mallon.

"Kamti, can you please go to the village of Humaita, tell our people we're here," Collins pleaded. Kamti persevered as he felt the need to bring this new information before his village head.

"I don't want to betray my people, but I'll speak with our village head again," said Kamti.

Later that day, Professor Hendrix began to express concern about Collins and Mallon's delay. It's evening and it's time to answer to the call of Ta-Piraha, the village head, but just before they leave, Collins and Mallon's absence from the pack is now very glaring, implying the professor isn't out of the woods yet.

"Collins and Mallon haven't returned from Manicore since yesterday," said Prof. Hendrix.

"Professor, maybe they're waiting for help to come," said Vera.

"They left here yesterday morning and haven't returned," said Prof. Hendrix. It isn't such a farce that Mallon and Collins didn't return immediately from Manicore, after all they're expected to come with as much help as possible. Sadly, the professor's hunch kept him hostage, and he just can't get his head around the nagging thought that his battles aren't over.

"Our going into the forest has put the professor under intense pressure," said Joel.

"That's what you expect to see when you go out with students," said Amanda. The distressed professor was irked by Amanda's careless comment because no degree of youthful exuberance should make him suffer as he just did.

"Do you mean you're all doing this to me on purpose?" the professor asked curiously. Beata didn't hesitate to put Amanda in her place, as fingers pointed at her and her boyfriend for precipitating this whole debacle in the first place. A silent war is brewing among the students particularly with Beata who's hopping mad at Kelvin for leading his course mates into this carbuncle of Satan, because the professor only permitted Kelvin to walk around the village and not to stray into the forest.

"Amanda that's rude, you must apologise to the professor, that remark is unacceptable," said Beata.

"Should we go and look for them?" asked Lee.

"I don't want more drama from you students, and I'm only trying to hold this together," said Prof. Hendrix.

"Professor, we're sorry about all this," said Joel. Amanda's abrasive and caustic comment has now made it look like the students deliberately engaged in some mischievous cat and mouse game against the professor, a needling feeling the professor finds difficult to shake off. It's now necessary to disabuse the professor's mind that none of this was intentional. It was quite a rambunctious moment as Beata used this as an opportunity to school Amanda on how to behave and that unwittingly set them on the war path.

"Professor, please, it wasn't intentional," said Terry.

"Professor, we're sorry, I realise I didn't choose my words properly. I was only referencing the boisterousness and youthful exuberance associated with young people but I mean no disrespect," said Amanda.

"Maybe after meeting with Ta-Piraha, we'll all trek to Manicore to search for Collins and Mallon," said Prof. Hendrix. They all set off for the palace to see the village head that's already waiting but continued their conversation on their way.

"But Professor, I can ride a bicycle to Manicore to fetch Mallon and Collins for you," said Lee.

"Don't worry, we'll all go together, I can't let any of you out of my sight because the odds are high and I can't risk it," replied Prof. Hendrix.

Not long after they set off for the palace and picking Noaita on the way, the professor and the students arrive the palace of the village head.

"Noaita, tell your friend that I'm happy he's able to reunite with his students that were lost in the forest," said Ta-Piraha.

Moments after welcoming the professor and his students, Ta-Piraha asked one of his guards to get the chief priest. The professor and the village head continued their conversation after sending for the chief priest.

"Tell him I said my students and I are very grateful to him, for his assistance," said Prof. Hendrix.

"Our chief priest said his students took something belonging to Ngala-na," said Ta-Piraha.

"I don't understand, is Ngala-na a snake? Because what they took is from a snake," said Prof. Hendrix. The chief priest walked into the conversation as he entered the palace.

"Noaita, tell him we don't know whether Ngala-na is a snake or not because we don't go into the forest in the days of the sun, and those are the days she comes out and as a result, we've never seen her," said Ta-Piraha. The professor was taken aback as he learnt that even the villagers have no idea of what their god looks like.

"I know my students took a diamond belonging to a snake and that's all, but I don't know about your god," said Prof. Hendrix. Funnily, Lee quickly interjected and urged the professor not to tell them about the diamond so they don't take it from them. He risked his life to get this trophy and he just can't hand it back in a whim.

Lee's effort to protect his trophy is now in jeopardy as professor Hendrix turned to him to make his stance on this matter clear.

"Lee, I can't tell lies, this is beyond what you think," said Prof. Hendrix. Their laughter surrounding their escape from the forest turned into smiles but unfortunately the smiles dissipated so quickly as every smiling face around suddenly turned into a frown because this mystery is already casting a long shadow on this research adventure.

Ta-Piraha turned to the chief priest to inquire from him about the personality of Ngala-na, and it has always been considered a taboo to do this.

"Is Ngala-na a snake? You know none of us has ever seen her," asked Ta-Piraha. The Chief Priest made some incantations and consultations, and after a while.

"Ngala-na is a spirit, and assumes the form of any animal it deems fit at any point in time but at this particular moment, yes, she's a snake. However, this is a secret kept away from generation to generation," said the Chief Priest. Noaita turned to the professor.

"The chief priest said it's a snake," said Noaita.

"Then Ngala-na must be the snake they took the diamond from," said Prof. Hendrix.

"Tell them Ngala-na is angry and there'll be consequences," said the Chief Priest. Unfortunately, the joy of the professor and his students seems to be short lived as their miraculous return isn't a miracle after all. Sadly, there doesn't seem to be an end in sight to their debacle as the chief priest has some bones to pick with them for stealing the forest's jewel.

"Tell him, the snake has returned to the river after losing her diamond, and that ends it," said Prof. Hendrix.

"Tell him, no, it isn't over, that Ngala-na will cause more destruction to our village as a result of his students' action," said the Chief Priest. Armed with the understanding that the chief priest is never wrong, and his words aren't just as smooth as butter but the truth, Ta-Piraha then turned to the chief priest in utter amazement.

"What do we do about this?" asked Ta-Piraha. "They have to stay within the village so we can appease the spirit of Ngala-na in three days' time," said the Chief Priest. The students became irate at the chief priest's pronouncement and things are about to get sour, and then ugly.

"This chief priest must be a jester," said Chantell. Kimberly turned to the distressed professor, and said it seems they're going to laugh a lot less with this unfolding drama. Vera couldn't help but exclaimed as she retorted that this research trip is now hellish, and urged the professor to get his act together because they need to get out of this village now, and run as fast as their legs can carry them. Johnny tried to tone the temperature down.

"Vera, don't say that. The professor is going above and beyond to get us all home in one piece," said Johnny.

"But we may need to go in search of our students who were lost in Manicore," said Prof. Hendrix.

"You all have to be here until the necessary rites are performed," said the Chief Priest.

"I can't stay here while my students remain missing somewhere, that's not going to happen," the professor threatened. The chief priest is trying to resolve the matter as amicable as he can, he then propose a second option.

"Ok, you can send only two people to search for them, while the rest of you will stay behind," said the Chief Priest.

"Professor, we're not going to fall for their game, we're leaving," Johnny retorted.

"Calm down, I'm trying to ensure your safety. I suppose you now see the trouble this walk into that forest without a guide is causing us?" said Prof. Hendrix.

Ta-Piraha turned to Noaita and urged him to inform his friends to remain and not leave the village, and "they shouldn't make us be hostile to them," said Ta-Piraha. The chief priest prides himself on his honesty and he isn't letting off on that at this point, as he held his ground as the mouthpiece of the gods.

"Tell him, we're passing the night here because it's late, but by tomorrow I'll go and look for my students," said Prof. Hendrix. After the back and forth, Professor Hendrix agreed to pass the night in the village of Humaita but insists on leaving the next morning to look for Collins and Mallon because there's not cat in hell's chance of staying in this village to perform some outrageous traditional rites when the whereabouts of two of his students remains unknown.

By the night of that day, by midnight to be precise, Ngala-na entered the village of Humaita just as the chief priest foretold, and this is happening for the first time in the history of that village. She destroyed most of the huts in the village in search for her diamond, which was still wrapped in Terry and Lee's clothing. That night, there was wailing, there was weeping, there was death, the oil lamps were lit but they couldn't give light and the village was pitch dark as the villagers were running helter-skelter in the midst of this confusion.

The Villagers ran for cover as they ran around taking shelter from whatever item they could find. Scream of "help, help! I can't find my child", was the cry all over the village.

"What have these students done? They've brought death unto us," cried the Village head. Strangely, as if Ngala-na want these natives to know she's the one punishing them, the moon suddenly appeared above them, and the pitch darkness disappeared as the moonlight took over. The palace guards took Ta-Piraha as they run for cover after his palace was smashed to rubble by Ngala-na. The professor and his students aren't spared from the ensuing confusion.

"Professor, let's get Noaita to tell us what is actually going on," said Johnny. The professor and his students rushed for cover, and sadly, Noaita is nowhere to be found because he's running as well.

"We seem to be responsible for the calamity of this peaceful community," said Beata.

Anteym and other hunters tried to ward off the monstrous snake but failed as they aren't any match for this monster.

"What's happening to our land?" cried Anteym. The calamity of this village is now common knowledge as the moonlight stood still and made Ngala-na visible to all eyes. Ngala-na decided not to deal death from a distance, but rather she came close and made herself quite visible so the villagers will know for sure that it's their god that is punishing them for their carelessness.

"Shush, look over there," said Prof. Hendrix in whispers, and pointing at a distance.

"That's a snake, and is that the snake they saw in the forest?" asked Johnny.

"You guys are right, and this snake is more than fourteen meters long," said Prof. Hendrix.

"A snake of this size is a danger to the human race," said Christian.

This creature is evasive and the professor is now convinced that this isn't just any snake but some demonic force in charge of this territory. What hope is there, now that this village is under siege? Ngala-na will wreak terror in this village and this horror isn't over until the natives of this village are put to flight for their negligence. The havoc wrecked by Ngala-na in a visit to this village is actually a premonition of what is to come, something quite unpleasant. Unfortunately, the misfortune of this village will grind on inexorably.

"This snake has smashed almost all the buildings in this village," said Johnny.

"The chief priest said there'll be more destruction, and it happened," said Lee.

"And I don't think this trouble is over," said Kelvin.

"Which means we brought all this trouble on these people," said Joel. The professor and his students spoke in whisper as they hid from the destruction that's been wrath before their eyes, and interestingly, they were spared from this destruction. The previous night, humans went for what belongs to the snake but this time it was the snake that came visiting.

Minutes later, Kualag, who is Anteym's younger brother and a hunter as well, and his son, Guagun, were swallowed by the snake. The snake left the village with only twenty huts standing out of a hundred and twenty-seven huts in the village.

"No, no! What's happening to us? " cried Anteym, as he watched the snake take his brother and nephew. Not long after Ngala-na left the village battered and without shape, the chief priest came to the palace to see Ta-Piraha, whose palace was also destroyed.

"I said there'll be more destruction," echoed the chief priest.

"These students have brought a great calamity upon us. Chief priest, what do we do?" asked Ta-Piraha. Even in the mist of his anger, the chief priest insists on observing the norm.

"You know I can't consult now, it's still dark," said the Chief Priest.

"But we're under attack, my village is under siege. Will you wait until we're all dead?" Ta-Piraha protested. The village head is best described as a moderate who thinks breaking with tradition to deal with imminent and active threat to life wouldn't be a sin, but it's not up to him to say what the gods expects in the current circumstance. It's obvious to the village head that the least of the chief priest's concerns is people thinking the worst of him, as he travails in standing in the gap for his people as the mouth piece of their gods. It's obvious that the village head doesn't want this ancient tradition to chafe his people under, but his hands are tied as the chief priest seems uncooperative.

"The snake has left, and I suggest we should go round to assess the level of human casualty," said the Chief Priest. "Ok, tomorrow morning I want to know what we should do, this calamity mustn't repeat itself," said Ta-Piraha.

"Ok, my king," said the Chief Priest.

Moments after their conversation, the chief priest, the village head, the hunters and the palace guards went round to assess the level of destruction left behind by Ngala-na. Sadly, the destruction on ground shows that Ngala-na didn't forget and didn't forgive the natives of this village for allowing some foreign rascals to desecrate her diamond.

The village head was left in shock when faced with the level of devastation left in the wake of Ngala-na's visit. He struggled to commit to memory all weeping and wailing of the previous night because they made him shudder, but blanking out that aspect of the trauma helped him to deal with the pressing matter at hand.

Obviously, Ngala-na doesn't do nice and she wouldn't need a colosseum to prove she's in charge here, and Ngala-na's wrath following these students' excesses could be the death knell for the village. He will do it anyway, and it doesn't matter whose ox is gored.

CHAPTER

SIX

4th of June – Fourth Day in Humaita

The next morning there was an unusual quiet in the village of Humaita as the people were trying to salvage what they could from the rubble, while some others were mourning their loss. The chief priest visited the palace to brainstorm with the village head as to the way out.

"My chief priest, you're welcome," said Ta-Piraha.

"My king, sorry about your palace, this is what the actions of a few callous students has resulted in," said the Chief Priest.

"I was mortified by the action of Ngala-na; this community has never seen anything like this since our ancestors lived here," said Ta-Piraha.

"Ngala-na is a god and the gods are never wrong. Four people died yesterday, the head hunter's brother, Kualag, and his son Guagun, were among the dead. My worry is now how to bring this destruction to an end", said the Chief Priest.

"Please, consult the gods and let us know what to do, to bring these destructions to an end," said Ta-Piraha.

This once bubbling village is now quiet, no cheers, no jeers, just utter silence as the villagers mourn and lick their wounds.

The chief priest made some incantations and consultations. My king, there is a solution, but it's a tough one," said the Chief Priest.

"What do you mean, how tough is it?" asked Ta-Piraha. At this point the village head is willing to do whatever it takes to spare his village the wrath of Ngala-na. It's now glaringly obvious that the gods must be appeased, but the question that begs to be answered is the village head's willingness to see this through.

"It depends on if you can go ahead with it, because if we don't the destruction will continue," said the Chief Priest.

"I could be meek, but not weak. Tell me what the gods have requested of us," said Ta-Piraha.

"The gods said we should sacrifice one of the students that caused us these troubles," said the Chief Priest. The village head expected the worst to be either sweet or sour, but sadly, it turned out to be bitter, and bitter only, and this time the chief priest is keen on suffering not the enemies of his gods to live.

"What? These people are our visitors, and I don't think its right to do such a thing," Ta-Piraha protested. This is a hard pill to swallow for the village head that initially showed willingness to go all the way. The choice now placed before the village head conflicts with his warm disposition towards foreigners.

"Their actions are sickening and disgusting and they don't deserve the pity you're showing to them," said the Chief Priest.

"Are you requesting that they should be sacrificed because you don't like them?" asked Ta-Piraha. The difficult request from the gods is about to precipitate into a quarrel between the two guardians of this village.

"You know that if I say contrary to what the gods have said then my life is in danger," said the Chief Priest.

"What precisely did they take from Ngala-na?" asked Ta-Piraha. The chief priest made some incantations and consultations.

"My king, they took her eyes" said the Chief Priest.

"That must be a horrible crime against Ngala-na," Ta-Piraha replied. Now that the broth is stirred, the peace enjoyed by this village for a thousand years has now been lost and Ngala-na has vowed to see to it that the natives are punished because the gloves are off.

"Now you know how bad the situation is," said the Chief Priest.

"What if the students return what they've taken? I think the sacrifice may not be necessary," Ta-Piraha proposed.

The Chief priest consulted the gods to make further inquiries.

"The sacrifice will still hold," said the Chief Priest. The position of the gods leaves the village head in a lurch as he's torn between keeping his subjects alive and hostility to his guests.

"Sacrificing a visitor has never been our practice. We don't hurt visitors and I suppose you're aware of our culture," Ta-Piraha said as he tries to drive his point home. The village did his best in his bid to enlighten the chief priest, as he sounded a note of caution that Ngala-na is wrath doesn't necessarily mean his village will suddenly turn into a mad house of barbarism where guests will lose their lives in the name of self-preservation.

The Chief priest wondered why they didn't act soon enough to have allowed this to escalate into an unmitigated disaster, and muttered saying there's no way they will come out of this smelling of roses. Ngala-na's terrifying campaign against this village meant these two have to agree on how to proceed.

The chief priest had to encourage the village head to be strong in his bid to stop him from droning on and on about how best to treat their supposed guests. Everything is as clear as mud so far, but this isn't the case for these vulnerable guests who expect their host to show them leniency rather than punished them for their missteps.

"My king, if we don't do this, we might face more destruction than what we've witnessed," said the Chief Priest. The village head became sober as he remained silent for a while wallowing in despair and defeat. After a moment of sober reflection, the village head opened his mouth as he turned to the chief priest.

"Ok, ask Anteym to gather the visitors and bring all of them to my palace," said Ta-Piraha.

"I'll send your guards to do that immediately, while I wait," said the Chief Priest.

While Anteym and Ta-Piraha's guards were going to fetch the professor and his students to the palace, the professor and his students were busy packing their things, preparing to leave the village for good in search for Collins and Mallon.

"Guys, be fast, we need to get to Manicore, and we need enough time to reason out what has happened to Mallon and Collins," said Prof. Hendrix.

"Professor, can we take Noaita with us to Manicore," to help us with translation?" asked Johnny.

"No, we don't need that. Manicore is a bigger village compared to this village, so we'll find people who understand and speak English," said Prof. Hendrix. Taking Noaita along represents a baggage that reminds this professor and his students of the terror associated with the village of Humaita, the ground zero of their proposed research expedition.

"The Professor is right; the hotel we lodged in Manicore, the guys there speak English," said Samantha.

"Professor, does it mean this research trip is over?" asked Tyler. The professor interjected and said his primary concern is to get all of them home safely, yet stressed that he still can't get his head around how his students walked seven kilometres into the deep end of the forest without a guide. The professor was still pained by the troubles he'd to go through, not only because his much anticipated research expedition has been ruined by his self-indulgent students, but because his frail health is now on the line.

"Professor, we're sorry about all this. I know we caused this," Lee apologised. The students managed to keep the sarcasm to an absolute minimum as they realised that Amanda's harmless banter raised eyebrows from some of their colleagues, and after all, manners don't cost anything.

"Now that I've found you guys, what about Mallon and Collins? Where are they?" asked Prof. Hendrix.

"Professor, but the village head said we shouldn't leave," said Kimberly. This is a jungle, and the professor understands that civility won't be the appropriate solution to jungle problems, yet Kimberly has just proposed civility, thinking it's the right and humane thing to do. Unsurprisingly, the professor seemed to have ditched civility in the bin, as he seems to be making a run for it because civility isn't the professor's priority.

"Just pack your bags, we're leaving in the next five minutes. What if that snake returns? What on earth can stop her?" asked Prof. Hendrix.

"But I think it'll be proper to ask Noaita to speak to the village head and to let him know we're leaving," Joel suggested.

While they were still talking, Anteym and the guards walked in on them. Unfortunately, language became a barrier as Noaita wasn't around to translate.

"You have to come with me," said Anteym. "What are you talking about? I can't understand you," said Prof. Hendrix.

"The village head wants all of you immediately," said Anteym. The professor and his students hesitated because they didn't understand what was being said. Anteym was irked by their dawdling, not realising the professor and his students didn't understand what's being said, and decided to apply some force to make them move. In a matter of seconds, a scuffle ensued.

"Stop! Don't force me, what's it? Get Noaita to interpret for us," the professor protested. Respite has now become a luxury Anteym can't afford as he's torn apart by the unending drama unfolding in different shapes and forms as the hour goes by.

Now that the kerfuffle seems to take a turn for the worst, Anteym heard the name of Noaita being mentioned by the professor and understood an interpreter was needed, he then asked one of the guards to get Noaita to help with interpretation.

"I'm beginning to have a negative feeling about this," said Joel.

"Professor, these people are becoming cynical, can we run?" asked Christian.

"That will not be a good idea, how far can you run? This is their forest," said Kelvin.

While the students are busy brainstorming and coming up with the weirdest of ideas on how to deal with the unfolding drama, Noaita arrived at the scene.

"It's good you're here, Noaita. Please tell him I said, where's he dragging us to?" asked Prof. Hendrix.

"Tell them, Ta-Piraha wants them," said Anteym.

"Tell him I said he shouldn't have been rough about it," the professor retorted.

Now that Ngala-na has sent a strong message of what's to come to the people of Humaita, tempers are flared and even the calmest of the villagers have lost their cool. The strongest man in the village, the head hunter, has born the wrath, as his brother and nephew were casualties of Ngala-na's vexation. Worse luck, there isn't any way out as the criminals responsible for this must pay, and pay dearly for their sins.

"Tell them they're wanted now, Ta-Piraha and the chief priest are waiting for them," said Anteym.

"Why will your chief priest be waiting for us?" asked Prof. Hendrix. The mention of the chief priest sent quivers in the professor who pretended to be calm so as not to make his students panic. The professor sensed trouble, particularly now that lives have been lost following the actions of his students.

"Tell them I said we should start going," said Anteym.

"Ok, let my students remain in the camp, while I go with them to the village head," the professor proposed.

"Tell him, Ta-Piraha wants all of them in his palace, and they should all come with me," said Anteym.

"Ok, let's go," said Prof. Hendrix.

The professor and his students abandoned what they were doing and followed Anteym to the palace. On reaching the palace, they met Ta-Piraha and the chief priest waiting as they walked into the palace.

"Noaita, please tell him I said I don't like this forceful summon, we're his guests," said Prof. Hendrix. The hope of leaving this village peacefully is now fading away and patience is now razor thin, as even the calm and collected professor is now beginning to lose his cool. The professor was profoundly affected by the aggression meted on them by these natives. This whole thing has suddenly become piping hot and it isn't giving the professor and his students the time needed to ruminate over their actions and experiences from the night before.

"Tell him if my guards were rough with him, we're sorry, just that we've an emergency at hand," said Ta-Piraha. The situation looked overly ambiguous even with the horror of the previous night firmly embedded in their minds. The blood is now hot on both sides, and the guardians of this village might find it difficult to justify this act of aggression as just a small sin for the greater good.

"Tell him I said, what emergency is he talking about? He should be quick about it, because we're leaving Humaita now," said Prof. Hendrix. The professor's posturing makes a good stunt but not good enough to resolve the brewing brouhaha precipitated by his students, and sadly, his posturing means nothing particularly in the middle of nowhere, far away from civilization.

"Tell him the emergency at hand is about what happened here last night," said Ta-Piraha.

"Tell him the snake has gone back to where it came from and we're leaving," the professor retorted.

"Tell him the snake will still come back and more of my people will die, and I don't want that," said Ta-Piraha. It's sad to say that what was down in the well always comes up in the bucket and what these students did in the forest, and away from the prying eyes of the natives the night before is now about to become common knowledge, as the gods laid it bare just as it is.

"Tell him I said, what has that got to do with us, what role do we play in it?" asked Prof. Hendrix.

"Yes, that's a good question; tell him our chief priest will speak with him about the rest," said Ta-Piraha.

The next line of conversation will be hard for the professor to take in, and the chief priest is best soothed for this because things won't be the same going forward as the hospitality is now moving fast into barbarism.

"Tell him I can't spend another day here waiting for him to per-form the rites he talked about," said Prof. Hendrix.

"Tell him everything will be sorted in the next one hour or even less than that, then they can leave," said the Chief Priest. The chief priest isn't just pulling new tricks off his sleeve, he's has chosen the easy way out where everyone will be better for it.

"Tell him I don't mind waiting about an hour for him to sort things out so we can leave," said Prof. Hendrix.

"Tell him the snake he saw last night isn't just a snake, that's Ngala-na, our god," said the Chief Priest. The professor tried to play down the assertion of the chief priest, by steering the conversation away from desecration and sacrilege to petty theft. "Tell him I said it was just a snake like any other snake, though, a big snake," said Prof. Hendrix. "Ngala-na is an embodiment of the beauty of our forest. That thing you called a snake isn't a snake, it's a spirit patrolling out forest in the form of a snake and it has lived over a thousand years. Mere snakes don't live that long, I suppose you're aware," said the chief priest. Please stop amplifying this myth, how do you know the snake has lived up to a thousand years, when yourself have barely lived seventy years?" asked Prof. Hendrix. Ta-Piraha quickly interjected and told the professor that his forefather, Nquira II stumbled into Ngala-na once in the forest but kept what he saw a secret. He then told them that Nquira II ruled the village of Humaita a thousand years ago.

As far these students are concerned, Ngala-na is a mosaic ancient creature that is nothing short of an embodiment of evil and wickedness existing as part snake and part god. The chief priest's perception of Ngala-na is miles away from what the students perceived the snake to be, he's convinced that this creature is the beauty of their forest, and Ngala-na is nothing short of the full embodiment of their god, and there isn't any part of that beast that's a snake, just that this creature has chosen to assume the nature of a snake at this moment in time.

"Tell him his students took the eye of Ngala-na," said the Chief Priest. Shocked at the direction of the conversation, the professor tried to put the conversation in the right perspective.

"Tell him my students didn't at any time touch the snake's eye, all they took was her diamond," said Prof. Hendrix.

"Tell him that diamond was her eye, because that was what she used to see and that was why she was here last night, she was looking for her eye," said the Chief Priest. This conversation has metaphorically turned into a rabbit hole with no end in sight, and pitifully, this chief priest has already-made answers for every single defence put forward by the professor.

"Tell him I said, if that'll resolve this issue peacefully, I'll hand him the diamond," said Prof. Hendrix.

"Tell him the diamond has been desecrated and cannot be accepted by Ngala-na that way," said the Chief Priest. These students have entered the forest and have encountered Ngala-na, and as it now stands these students have seen so much that there is to see in their short stay in this forest. Unfortunately, they can't unsee what they've seen in the last two nights, neither can they undo what they've done. This is because they're now the only privileged few who know the animal whose form Ngala-na currently assumes before it paid the unscheduled visit to the village the previous night in search for her eyes.

This should've been success that's worth celebrating but not until the Chief Priest considers their act of brigandage as a good omen, but unfortunately, it isn't. They now have to bear the consequence of their exuberance, and unfortunately, the price is costly and they might have to pay with their lives. The professor then looked at Noaita and asked him to inquire from the Chief priest who seem to be running the show, what he suggests they do since they don't want the diamond.

"Tell him those students that went into the forest should come this way to my left," said the Chief Priest. The chief priest decided to sort the students into two groups, those that entered the forest to the left and those that didn't, remain on the right. Things are moving so fast, at a pace faster than the professor could keep up with, and the professor quickly asked the Chief Priest why he's sorting his students into two groups.

"What does he want to do to them?" the professor asked in desperation.

"Tell him I'm doing nothing to them, after all, we're all here," said the Chief Priest. The professor concurred and allowed the sorting to go ahead.

"Ok guys, you can sit that way," said Prof. Hendrix.

"Professor, why're you giving in to their demands?" asked Tyler.

"We're all here and I'm with you in this," the professor assured.

After the seven students moved to the left-hand side of the chief priest, the chief priest casted a lot on their behalf. Surprised at what's going on, the professor quickly turned to Noaita and asked him to inquire from the chief priest what it was he's doing.

"Tell your friend I'm casting a lot on their behalf," said the Chief Priest. The professor sensed that things are beginning to get doggy, as this whole expedition is quickly turning into quicksand that's unravelling in multiple dimensions. The unease in the air inside this palace is palpable enough to be cut with a knife. Arguably, these students might not leave this village in one piece, particularly now that they're caught in the brambles of greed and entrapment.

"Tell him I said, why is he casting a lot? What's he going to do with the outcome of the lot?" asked Prof. Hendrix.

"Tell him I said they can cast the lot themselves, and all we need is one of them to perform the rites necessary to quench the anger of our gods," said the Chief Priest. Sadly, in the current circumstance the chief priest has inexhaustible resources to make things go his way without expending tremendous energy.

"Tell him none of my students will perform any rites, we're leaving now," the professor retorted in an angry outburst.

Unfortunately, the lot fell on Kimberly, and the chief priest singled her out, and released the rest. "Tell him they can leave, the gods have chosen her," said the Chief Priest as he pointed his finger at

Kimberly. The furious professor stood up from his seat and stood between Kimberly and the chief priest.

"Tell him I said she isn't performing any rites, and we're leaving here now," said Prof. Hendrix.

To the amazement of the professor and his students, things became feisty as chief priest ordered the guards to drag Kimberly away. The students and their professor tried to resist but they were outnumbered and overpowered by the guards and hunters present. Kimberly cried and screamed uncontrollably, throwing her fist against the air as she's being dragged away to one side of the hut, and kept in holding.

"No! Why me? Let me go. Joel, don't let them do this to me," she cried. The professor and his students tried to retrieve Kimberly, but they were stopped by the hunters and guards who overpowered them.

"Tell him to stop this; we want to leave this village now," said Prof. Hendrix as he pleads with the chief priest.

"Tell them to leave if they want, we've got who we wanted for the rites," said the Chief Priest.

"Tell him we can't leave without her, ask him how long it'll take her to perform the rites and join us," asked Prof. Hendrix. The chief priest gave the professor the grime truth about what the rites entails and this can't be anything but the height of barbarism. Wallowing in self-pity won't help the professor at this point, particularly now that things have just turned grim and gritty.

"Tell him she will not be joining them again, they can leave," said the Chief Priest. The professor and his students were gripped with confusion as they couldn't get their head around what's happening to them.

They tried in their numbers to release Kimberly but failed as the villagers are armed and they outnumbered the students. If Kimberley like she can cry a river, her tears meant nothing to this chief priest who is convinced that he has been tasked by the villagers to deployed damage control to conciliate the gods.

Out of desperation the professor turned to Noaita to plead with the village head who's seated and observing the proceedings.

"Please tell him I know he's a man of integrity, that he shouldn't do this to us," said Prof. Hendrix.

"Tell him I said I'm sorry, that's the demand of the gods and I must protect my people," said Ta-Piraha.

"Tell him I want to know what's he going to do with the girl? Because we aren't leaving her here," said Prof. Hendrix. As far as this chief priest is concerned the professor is sounding like a DJ in a local radio and seems not to realise, he's in for a long ride.

The chief priest interjected as Noaita asked the question.

"Tell him he has to, because she isn't coming back, unless he wants to replace her with someone else," said the Chief Priest. Kimberly cried out in her helplessness, as she turned to Noaita.

"No! Noaita, please do something, help us, beg him," cried Kimberly. Armed with the realisation that they're in the middle of nowhere and help isn't coming. The helpless professor decided that it's best he pay the price for his students' indiscretion by trading himself to secure his students safety.

"Give me your word that if I replace her for you to do whatever to me, you'll let all my students go out of your village unharmed," said Prof. Hendrix. Sadly, the professor who hadn't the foggiest idea of the chief priest's semantics didn't fit the mould, and can't be of any help to Kimberly. The chief priest's intentions remained shrouded in mystery, and soon those intentions will be laid bare.

"Tell him he can't replace her because he wasn't among those that went into the forest and angered our gods," said the Chief Priest. Kimberly continued crying uncontrollably and her fiancé, Joel, watched helplessly and suddenly decided that if the professor can't save her, maybe he should. Joel then jumped up from his seat to the amazement of all present.

"She's my fiancée, can I replace her? Can I take her place? Ask him, I say, ask him," Joel pressed Noaita to ask the Chief Priest.

"Joel, calm down, there may be another way out of this," said Prof. Hendrix. Replacing one student with another still implies that the professor is unable to save all his students. The professor was in great shock as his inability to rescue his student left him in quite a pickle, which he finds distressing. The blood rush to Joel's head hasn't abated and he remained quite agitated and confused.

"No Professor, that's my fiancée in there, I must do something. They better take me instead," said Joel.

"Yes, you can," said the Chief Priest who doesn't want to be perceived as being quite unreasonable. The chief priest then swapped Kimberly for Joel but just as the guards attempted to take Joel away, Lee stood up in haste.

"All these people are innocent, all this is happening because I went for that diamond," said Lee. The drama continued, and it's now glaringly obvious that a life must be taken to cure this problem.

"Lee, it's my fiancée we're talking about here, just let me do this for my fiancée," said Joel.

Lee turned to the guards, and pressed on them to let Joel go.

"Let him go, take me, let me pay the price for my actions. I'm the cause of all this. Just tell my dad I'm sorry and tell my mum I love her," said Lee.

Lee wept as he handed himself over to the guards, Kimberly and Joel returned to the pack as Lee was taken away.

"What are they going to do to Lee?" asked Vera.

The professor and the students decided to hang around in the village of Humaita to see if there was any possibility of securing

Lee's release. Meanwhile, Collins and Mallon remained locked up in the cell in the village of Parana for the third day. Mallon was in no mood for pleasantries the moment Kamti walked in to check on the two prisoners.

"Kamti, what are you doing here?" asked Mallon.

"My friends, what do you mean?" asked Kamti.

"Don't call us your friends, you're of no use to us, and you're just a waste of space," Mallon retorted.

"I've tried to secure your release but the village head refused, though I'll keep trying," said Kamti.

"I begged you to go to the village of Humaita and let our people know we're locked up here," said Collins. Since effort to secure the sympathy of the village head has failed, the only option left will be to inform the professor that his students were locked up in Parana.

"You know I'll not be able to do that, and I wouldn't want to incur the wrath of my people," said Kamti. Hurtling down to the village of Humaita isn't among the cards on the table for Kamti, and he isn't willing to play this ball because his fingers could get burnt.

"Kamti, you have to take this food back, I'm not interested," said Mallon. Kamti became emotional in a show of sympathy, even though he's still helpless in this matter.

"My friends you have to eat, because you're already looking pale," Kamti pleads.

Either way, Kamti remains the only hope to freedom for Collins and Mallon, as he's the only means of communication and the only person sympathetic towards their ordeal.

"Kamti, please just keep trying to see if you can convince your village head for us. Though, get us more of those fruits, we can sustain on that," said Collins.

"Ok, let me go and get as much of those fruits as I can," said Kamti.

This case remains open in the mind of those involved, and Kamti remained hopeful that his pleadings will soon touch the soft side of his village head, but hope on the village head's magnanimity is fading fast, and then Mallon decided it's best to turn his sight to the professor.

"Why has the professor forgotten us? I never expected he could do this to us," said Mallon.

"Let's just be strong, because we don't even know what the situation is in the village of Humaita," said Collins. No one is spared the short end of the stick as this research expedition turned sour. Sad to say, everyone is on their own at the moment fighting their battle and Mallon need to come to terms with his own reality.

"But it'll cost him less stress to come and get us out, than continue with whatever he's doing," said Mallon.

"Don't you think they might be searching for us already? They might think we're in Manicore," said Collins.

It's not new to Collins that Mallon is a cry baby who complains about anything and everything. Just days ago, even before this research expedition kicked off, Mallon was complaining about the fact that he doesn't have enough time to complete his assignment for one of the courses.

He complained about the lecturers' lack of understanding and compassion, he also complained about the university authority's ineptitude that allows his lecturer get away with it, and complained against the government for not doing a proper monitoring on how the university treats its students. He nagged and nagged, and suddenly said he can't wait to leave London, then began to complain about the noise in the city, particularly the police sirens that do his head in.

"Where then do you want to live, the penitentiary?" Asked Collins.

"Of course not, who said I don't like it in London? I still like it here," said Mallon.

Back in the village of Humaita, the professor and his students returned without Lee, he then asked his students to remain in their huts to keep them out of harm's way. The professor went into his bag to get his licensed pistol and went to the chief priest without the knowledge of his students to see if he could forcefully secure Lee's release but decided to get Noaita on his way.

"Please come with me," said Prof. Hendrix.

"Where are you going?" asked Noaita. "Just come with me because I'll need you to interpret for me," said Prof. Hendrix. But Noaita sensed the professor's visit to the chief priest without his student isn't in good faith, because it isn't long that the professor and his students returned to their huts.

"Ok, but are you going to see the Chief priest?" asked Noaita.

"Yes, as you can see I'm headed in that direction," the professor retorted. They arrived at the shrine where Lee was being held awaiting the ritual. The chief priest who didn't want anyone standing in his way, was busy humming his traditional incantations associated with performing traditional rites for their gods, even as he mourns Lee's death in advance. Just as the professor drew closer, the chief priest quickly turned around and stood in the professor's way.

"What has he come to do? I've told him he can't get him back," said the Chief Priest. The professor dipped his hand into his pocket and brought out his pistol and pointed it at the chief priest.

"Tell him to release the boy now," said Prof. Hendrix. Noaita exclaimed at the sight of a gun pointed at the chief priest.

"Awe! He said you should let the boy go, or he'll shoot you," said Noaita. The chief priest doesn't seem perturbed at the professor's threat.

"Noaita, tell him pointing a gun at me will not help him, it'll only put him and his students in danger," said the Chief Priest.

The professor turned to Lee who was tied up yet still weeping like a baby. These students have seen a great deal of sorrow since they stepped on the blood rock, and their troubles don't seem to be going away soon.

"Lee, are you ok?" asked Prof. Hendrix.

"Professor, I'm not ok, what's going to happen to me?" cried Lee.

"Tell your priest I'll shoot him if he doesn't untie the boy," said Prof. Hendrix. The chief priest remained unperturbed as he continued to prepare the concoction for his sacrifice.

"Noaita, tell him I said he should put the gun down and walk away, and I'll pretend he never pointed a gun at me," said the Chief Priest.

"Tell him I'll shoot him and his gods won't be able to save him," said Prof. Hendrix.

"Tell him his time is up, he should turn around and see what's behind him," said the Chief Priest. The professor turned around and saw five hunters pointing arrows at him. "What's going on?" asked the horrified Professor. The professor is now in harm's way and could become an additional casualty, Noaita decided to step in immediately to save his professor friend.

"Chief priest, please, let him go, he'll put the gun down, just that he's responsible for these students and doesn't know how to communicate this to the boy's parents," pleads Noaita. The professor refused to give in, as he's bent on taking Lee with him, and how he intends to achieve this leaves much to be desired because this chief priest's casual savagery has now been weaved into the tradition of this peaceful village.

"Noaita, tell them to lay down their weapons, or I'll shoot their chief priest," the professor retorted.

"My visitor, bring your hand down. Can't you see you won't leave here alive if you shoot that gun, and how can you help the boy if you're dead?" asked Noaita. It didn't take long before the professor realised this move is self-defeating, and he'd no choice but to bow to the fact that he can only be of help to Lee if he's alive. After all, a living dog is better than a dead lion.

This isn't the case of old dogs reassuringly using old tricks, the chief priest is a different horse and applying the old technique of threats will fail woefully, particularly now that the professor and his student are so damn gullible.

This Chief priest who is now adorned in his traditional regalia and looking his best for the occasion at hand, will ensure that this rascal of a professor will not interfere with the traditional rites of Lee's sacrifice to his god.

"Ok," said Prof. Hendrix. He brought down his hand and the hunters seized the gun from the professor, and sadly, his glimmer of hope fades away just like that before his eyes.

This professor isn't lacking in bravery and neither is he lacking in determination, but his inability to secure his students' release meant the professor is now looking like a cowboy lost in the midst of the herd he's meant to control. He'd no choice at this point than to choose the path of cool heads.

"Tell him I've nothing against him but he should go, and I forgive him," said the Chief Priest.

Arguably, even as the chief priest works doubly hard to make sure no one steals his thunder, he can bet on it that allowing the professor the privilege of walking away unhurt will give him the breather that allows him to continue fighting on until he secures Lee's release.

"Tell him, before I leave here, I would like to know what he's going to do to the boy," said Prof. Hendrix.

"We'll prepare him as a sacrifice for the snake," said the Chief Priest. On hearing the chief priest barbarous intention, Lee shivered uncontrollably and peed in his pants.

"No, no. Professor, I can't end up in the belly of that monster, no, not in the belly of that thing," Lee cried.

"Tell him we'll need to spend some time with him, at least to bid him farewell," said Prof. Hendrix.

The chief priest's benignity leaves much to be desired and while his guests likened his disposition to a dog with a bone. The villagers didn't see him as a dog with a bone, but rather they likened him to be more of a Rottweiler protecting his god. At the moment he has no intention of placing his foot on the brakes until Lee finds himself in the belly of Ngala-na.

"Tell him they are free to spend some time with him to wish him goodbye; they can even be there because the sacrifice will be taking place in the next one hour," said the Chief Priest. No one hears of their death discussed in this manner and remain calm and collected. Unfortunately, crying his eyes out is the only option left to Lee.

"Ok, my students and I will be back," said Prof. Hendrix. The professor returned to the camp empty handed without Lee, broken, defeated, and in tears. The students have also been in tears since Lee was taken from them. Terry noticed from afar that their professor is equally in tears as he walks back to his hut.

"Guys, the professor seems to be crying," said Terry.

"He has been crying since they took Lee away," said Vera. Joel has been praying since Lee was taken, but his strength is failing him as he could only mutter his prayers.

"Let's go to him, and find out what he knows that we don't," said Amanda. The students went into the professor's hut and actually found him crying.

"Professor, where are you coming from?" asked Vera.

"Did they promise to give him back to us?" asked Tyler. "I tried to release him but I failed and they've taken my gun," Prof. Hendrix retorted. The professor cried the more, and this got his students to be more emotional, each person weeping and no one could comfort the other. This village has suddenly turned these wild and fearless students into complete morons.

"Professor, did you go to the chief priest? What are they going to do to Lee?" asked Terry.

"They're sacrificing him to that snake," said Prof. Hendrix. The gut-wrenching revelations caused the students' stomach to churn.

"Jesus!" exclaimed Joel. "What!" Amanda exclaimed.

"No, they can't do this!" Terry exclaimed. The distressed professor and his students spent some time weeping, yet came to terms with Lee's fate and continued brainstorming on the way forward. "Though they said we can see Lee and spend some time with him, before they do whatever they want with him," said Prof. Hendrix. Lee's dad is a military General who obviously could turn this forest into a desert, but has no knowledge of his sons' present debacle in the hands of these Amazonian natives. His son is the middle of nowhere, and had to rely on the support of his friends to stay alive.

"Professor, why don't we go to Manicore to get help? There's a police station there," asked Beata.

"By the time we get to Manicore and come back they would've killed him," said Prof. Hendrix.

"But we can get the police here in about two or three hours," said Samantha.

"That'll be too late, because they're doing whatever they intend to do within the hour," said Prof. Hendrix. Some of the students remained hopeful even in the mist of this hopelessness, while others lick their wounds in advance.

"So, we've to be here to do whatever we can for him, to see if we can secure his release," said Christian.

The professor and his students then hurriedly left their huts and went to see Lee where he was tied up in the chief priest's shrine, and funnily, Lee cheered up the moment his course-mates came calling. "Why're you all crying? Your tears are increasing my fear of dying," asked Lee.

"Why wouldn't we cry? I talked you into doing this," Terry tearfully said.

"No, grabbing the diamond from the snake was my idea, it's obvious I'm going to die today, let me face death with courage," said Lee.

"What do you mean by that? This isn't a circus show," said Kelvin.

"I mean you guys should keep your emotions to yourself because I need courage to go through this," said Lee. This courage seems short lived, and it's obvious that no amount of courage will help any mortal man remain sane after beholding Ngala-na, because this monster is something outside the ordinary.

"Don't talk like that, Lee, death isn't a thing to joke about," said Amanda.

"Do I have a way out? No, I just have to face it," said Lee. Now that Lee seem ready to face the inevitable, yet wished his death will be painless, Joel on the other hand felt it's appropriate for Lee to make his way right with God.

"Lee, this could be your only opportunity to make your way right with your maker," said Joel. Most of the students present were left hopping mad at Joel as they considered it lunacy for a dying man to be bothered in this manner. The chief priest didn't really bother about whatever the students do with themselves provided Lee remains in chains.

"Joel, why not let him be?" asked Tyler.

"No, this is Lee's chance to make things right with God, so if he dies today he'll make heaven," said Joel. Even Joel's fiancée wasn't on his side either, because she considered Joel's request to be an overreach but Joel wasn't deterred by this strong opposition.

"Joel, I don't think this is the right time for you to do this," said Kimberly. Lee tried to stay courageous, yet continues to shudder even as his conversation with his friends persists. "Allow Lee to answer for himself. Are you ready for this, Lee, and do you have faith?" asked Joel.

"Yes, yes, yes. After all, I've nothing to lose and everything to gain," said Lee. Joel didn't hesitate to lead Lee to Christ. "Lee, repeat after me. Lord Jesus, I come to you today a sinner, I accept you as my lord and saviour. Wash me of my sins, cancel my name from the book of death, and write my name in the book of life," said Joel. Lee repeated after Joel, crying. But in a dramatic twist of faith Lee felt some inner peace in the face of imminent death. "Thank you, Joel, for giving me this opportunity. My faith is in God now," said Lee. The professor still felt the need to try one last time to secure Lee's release.

"Lee, I'll go and see the village head to see if I can convince him to stop this madness," said Prof. Hendrix.

"Professor, let's all pray for Lee," said Joel. "I can't, I'm an Atheist, I don't believe in that, but those of you that believe should just keep praying," said Prof. Hendrix.

"I'm and not a Christian either, so I don't believe in your prayers," said Tyler.

"All of you should pray to God, for me, and Tyler, I want you to join in," said Lee.

"Take this Bible with you, hold it to your chest at all times," said Joel. Lee is in chain and can't hold a bible to his chest.

"But my hands are tied, and I can't hold it," said Lee.

"Ok put it in your pocket," said Joel.

Since there isn't a way to hand a bible to Lee, Joel decided to dip the bible in Lee's pocket. After all, it's just a pocket bible.

"At least, I can face death now," Lee said and began to weep again.

Terry has been crying all along, he was held bound by the guilt of being the main enabler of Lee's action, even with words of consolation from friends, it remained difficult for Terry to put himself together. Friends are concerned he's making the whole thing more emotional and difficult for Lee. Tyler went to him trying to make him stop but that seem not to have worked.

Suddenly, amid tears, Terry began singing the song "It's So Hard to Say Goodbye to Yesterday" by Boyz II Men.

How do I say goodbye to what we had?
The good times that made us laugh
Outweigh the bad

I thought we'd get to see forever
But forever's gone away
It's so hard to say goodbye to yesterday

I don't know where this road
Is going to lead
All I know is where we've been
And what we've been through

And if we get to see tomorrow
I hope it's worth all the wait
It's hard to say goodbye to yesterday

And I'll take with me the memories
To be my sunshine after the rain
It's so hard to say goodbye to yesterday

And I'll take with me the memories
To be my sunshine after the rain
It's so hard to say goodbye to yesterday

Terry's move seems to have taken his colleagues by surprise, and while some tried to stop him for making the whole thing more emotional and difficult for them, he refused to stop and insisted he's mourning Lee, and that's his own way of saying goodbye to a dear friend.

Even as some tried to shut him up, saying this song is uncalled for, and that he shouldn't mourn a friend who is alive and standing right in their mist. All Terry could say was that Lee is dead, and if he isn't dead now, he soon will be. He sang louder even as he cried the more, but in no uncertain terms told his friends that his singing is nothing but a funeral service for Lee.

Terry however continued singing and why some took objection to his action, Tyler joined, and one after another, they each joined, and it didn't take long before all the students began singing goodbye song to Lee.

The cold hand of death awaits Lee on the other side to snatch Lee away, and what other way to release a friend to the great beyond if not to mourn him, particularly when his parents and relatives aren't there to give him a befitting funeral.

The professor watched helplessly as the students did their own thing. Lee is now among the privilege few to have their funeral ceremony happening right before their eyes while they are still alive, and what makes this ceremony unique was the fact that there was no eulogy, no snacks, no drinks, no walking around coffins, just weeping for the poor boy.

This time, no cremation, and no internment, just the belly of Ngala-na will decide what happens to Lee's carcass because his Lee's life will be snuffed out like a candlewick in a matter of seconds.

Not long after Joel dipped the bible into Lee's pocket, and this unplanned funeral service ended that the chief priest came with his henchmen to take Lee away because it's time for the long awaited ritual. The professor quickly turned to Noaita as the hunters took Lee away, and led him down the forest path like a sheep led to the slaughter. Funnily, what started as plain stupidity has suddenly morphed into horror and barbarism.

"Noaita, where's he taking him to?" asked Prof. Hendrix.

"Tell him we're taking him to the forest, he can come and watch how the sacrifice is done if he likes," said the Chief Priest.

Unsurprisingly, the eleventh hour is over and now the twelfth hour is here, and Lee is now being led to the alter for the sacrifice. The professor and the students hurriedly rushed to Ta-Piraha in a last ditch effort to secure Lee's release and save the day. Sadly, the hands of the village head are tied in this matter, as he finds himself between a rock and a hard place.

"Noaita, tell him these students are in my custody and I can't go home without him," said Prof. Hendrix.

"Tell him there's nothing I can do, we need to save our people from the wrath of the gods," said Ta-Piraha. The professor has no choice but to resort to threat of what will befall this village if they kill Lee. "Tell him if they do this, our government will rain fire on this community, and his people won't be spared either," said Prof. Hendrix.

"Tell him we want to quench the wrath of our gods before we think of what his government will do or won't do," said Ta-Piraha. As far as this village is concerned, the fear of Ngala-na is the beginning of wisdom, because this snake could wipe out their existence.

"Noaita, tell him we'll give him money or even buy him a car, whatever he wants from us," said Prof. Hendrix. Time is now a luxury, and the already exhausted professor has no choice but to resort to making promises since all effort to secure Lee's release has largely failed. The professor isn't being careless in a manner of frivolous spending that will leave a serious dent in his pocket, he'd no choice but to do all he could to secure Lee's release. Sadly, this village's eccentricity has become their guests' undoing.

"Noaita, please tell him I'll give him plenty of money, I'll buy him a car if he let the boy go.

"Tell him I'm not a selfish ruler, my people's interest comes before mine," said Ta-Piraha.

"Tell him he's the head of this village and not the chief priest, why can't he just help us?" asked Prof. Hendrix. It's just sad to say that the chief priest has the final say in matters of this nature, and the village head believes in him because he was never wrong. It's now obvious that Lee's fate is now in the hands of the gods, and it's now at the pleasure of the gods to do to Lee as they deem fit.

"Tell him, the chief priest only says the truth, and he's only performing his duty," said Ta-Piraha.

This Village head is scarcely reticent when matters of this nature are on the table but this time it doesn't matter whose ox is gored, he's has chosen to stay mum to allow tradition run its course.

"Guys, let's trail the chief priest, and see what they're doing to Lee. Since the village couldn't help, the professor and his students left the palace in haste for the forest trailing the chief priest, the hunters with him, and Lee to the point of the sacrifice.

"Professor, I don't think it's a good idea to watch my course mate being sacrificed to a snake because the picture will remain in my memory, and it'll haunt me for life," said Amanda.

"But we can't just abandon him and go our way, that won't be fair," said Terry.

"I must follow Lee till the end to see what actually happens to him," said Prof. Hendrix. Even as the heart broken professor remained determined to see this through to the end, those who can't withstand the horror decided it's best to stay away and possibly spectate from afar.

Sacrifices of this significance aren't done hastily, and they're carefully choreographed to avoid provoking the gods further. It must be led by the little village priestess, a virgin, who also reports to the chief priest. She must lead the procession, chanting praise to Ngala-na, the guardian of their village, the god of fruitfulness and harvest, and the giver of life.

"Professor, are you aware someone like me might die of heart attack in this forest after watching that?" asked Amanda.

"You're right, Amanda. Those who can't see this till the end will stay some distance away, while some of us will go closer," the professor proposed.

"Don't worry Amanda, some students will join you and wait some distance away from the scene," said Kelvin. Amanda held tightly onto Kelvin while looking the opposite direction away from Lee, as she couldn't behold the sight of that snake in day light.

"Guys, watching this horror is heart wrenching for me, but if I don't, how do I explain Lee's death to the school authority?" said Prof. Hendrix.

"Amanda, let's wait here; those of you that can't get any closer should wait here," said Kelvin. Kelvin and all the ladies waited, except Kimberly who chose to draw closer because she owed it to Lee for taking her place after the lot fell on her.

"I can't stay behind, I'll follow him till the end. He took my place, and I should've been the one dying," she said. Kimberly never stopped weeping since Lee gave himself up, and even when all hope is now lost, the professor is still bent on daring to rescue Lee even in this last minute.

"Let's get closer to the scene and hide to see if there could be any slight opportunity to rescue the boy," said Prof Hendrix.

After about two hours the chief priest and his team arrive the bank of the River Maici. The chief priest kept Lee on top of the blood rock that was situated just by the bank of river Maici. He cut himself and some blood came out of his finger, which dripped right into a can of fatty concoction. He mixed his blood with the fatty concoction, then rubbed it all over Lee, and threw some inside the river, then minutes later, the river rumbled and the chief priest and his team ran as far as they could, and hid themselves somewhere.

Not long from that moment, Ngala-na came out of the river, and came straight for Lee. The monster is quite a sight to behold, dam ugly, and evil, and it's quite understandably that Lee peed on himself the moment this monster presented herself in full glare, Ngala-na is never a thing any mortal being should behold. And in a twinkle of an eye, she swallowed Lee and went back to the river. The sight of what just happened greatly distressed the professor and his students, Kimberly lost her balance following the horror she just saw and fell flat on her face.

"Is this really happening?" the professor cried. Kimberly, who's the only lady that drew closest to the scene of the ritual needed to be revived after a temporal loss of consciousness. Immediately she got herself, she quickly, turned to her fiancée.

"Joel, can you see that? Lee is gone, he's dead," Kimberly cried before tipping over again. The professor and Joel rushed to help Kimberly up for the second time.

"I pushed him into doing this, Lee's blood is now on me for life," said Terry. All those that saw what happened cried. Even some of the hunters with the chief priest consigned their initial animosity towards Lee to the bin as they become emotional, because no one deserves to die in this manner. The professor cried as he couldn't hold back his emotion.

"I tried to save him, but I failed," said Prof. Hendrix.

Immediately Ngala-na swallowed Lee and returned to the river, a big battle ensued in the belly of the beast. The darkness in the evil inside Ngala-na battled with the light inside the bible in Lee's pocket. This whole battle is now happening inside Ngala-na and the river rumbled much more than it ever did, and fifteen minutes later Ngala-na rushed out of the river and hastily spewed Lee out of her mouth, and then went back into River Maici. The professor and his students who were still in shock mourning and comforting each other over Lee's death, were returning to the village when they were attracted by the noise and then rushed back and watched in surprise as Lee was vomited by Ngala-na. They ran to Lee, who wasn't breathing, and with slimy stuff all over his body.

The professor quickly checked for a pulse and to see if Lee is still breathing.

"Oh no!" said the professor.

"Is he breathing?" asked Johnny. "No, he isn't, let me deliver CPR immediately," said the professor. The professor and his students continued with the CPR, hoping that Lee will come back.

"Lee, Lee, come on. Wake up," said Terry. The chief priest was surprise as Ngala-na rejected the sacrifice but rushed to see to it that Lee isn't breathing.

"Let him be. He's dead, and he's supposed to be dead," said the Chief Priest. Joel continued praying even as his mates delivered the CPR.

"You're a liar, he isn't supposed to be dead, you just want him dead," said Terry. The professor continued without letting go.

"Come on boy, come back," the professor cried. "Lee, come on," Joel cried, even as he continued to pray.

"Come on boy, this is your second chance. Come on," screamed Prof. Hendrix. After about five minutes of persistence, Lee came back and joy erupted. Kimberly called out to the other group of students watching from afar.

"Guys, come over here. Lee is alive; he made it," said Kimberly.

The chief priest became surprised that Lee made it back to life but couldn't get his head around why his oracle didn't tell him Ngala-na will reject the sacrifice.

"Does it mean Ngala-na didn't like the sacrifice?" asked the muttering chief priest. The professor turned to the chief priest in excitement but to the disappointment of the Chief Priest.

"At least you will let us be, now that your snake returned him herself," said Prof. Hendrix.

"Where am I, and where is he?" Lee asked, the moment he opened his eyes.

"Where's who? I'm not following you!" exclaimed Prof. Hendrix. "The man that came out of my pocket to save me while I was in the belly of that snake," said Lee. Lee's assertion left the professor and his course mates rattled.

"You mean a man came out of your pocket to save you?" the professor asked curiously.

"Yes, but it looked like the bible Joel gave me actually turned into that man, I just can't explain," said Lee.

"Oh my God! That's Jesus, he just saved you," said Joel.

"What do you mean Jesus saved him? Lee was in the belly of a beast and can't see clearly, let's not rush into a premature judgement," said Tyler. Terry then said he know people use the bible to ward off vampires but for the bible to turn into a man is something out of the blue. Terry's knowledge of Lee as someone who doesn't blow smoke meant Lee isn't telling lies.

"Tyler, what are you saying, and you think I made this up? I'm miffed by your comment," said Lee. Joel seems not to like Tyler's view of Lee's testimony.

"Lee just told you the bible saved him, the bible is the word of God and the word of God is Jesus. Please don't trivialise Lee's miracle," Joel retorted.

"Ok, ok, my hands are up, please accept my apology," said Tyler.

"Then that's strange, I'm glad to have you back, either way," said Prof. Hendrix.

While this conversation was going on, the river suddenly rumbled, and rumbled, and suddenly the professor and his students rushed back and took Lee to safety as they saw Ngala-na crept out of the river, Ngala-na came out from the river in pain, like a choking animal, and began to wriggle herself. While this was going on, both the professor and his students, and even the chief priest and his team ran further away from the scene for cover. After about thirty minutes of intense struggling, Ngala-na went on top of the blood rock by the bank of River Maici and died. Sadly, the death of Ngala-na was a horror to behold, and funnily, the trees in the forest were spared this time as Ngala-na limited his last fight on top of the blood rock.

"Ooh, the snake is dead. Lee has killed a god!" exclaimed Terry. There was screams the moment Ngala-na laid motionless and died. Moments of intense grief has suddenly turned into cheers.

"Lee is the only person to steal a diamond from a god and kill the god two days later," said Tyler. The chief priest was taken aback to see his ancient god destroyed by a higher power he'd no knowledge of.

"They've killed Ngala-na, I never saw this coming. These people are evil, let them leave our village," said the Chief Priest.

"What did the boy do to Ngala-na?" the Chief Priest queried further, in a bid for answer.

"Maybe he has a higher power we do not know about," said Anteym the chief hunter. "Noaita, tell them to take their things and leave our village immediately," said the Chief Priest.

"Tell him we're about to do just that," said Prof. Hendrix. The professor and his students hurried back to their huts and concluded their parking with the speed of light.

Joel later called Lee aside to hear a bit more detail about his miraculous escape that resulted in Ngala-na spewing him. Lee didn't hold back to Joel whom he considered the architect of his survival. He then narrated that not long after Ngala-na swallowed him, there were echoes of mercy that kept ringing out and reverberating, and it didn't take long, echoes of the word mercy, mercy, saturated the belly of that monster. Suddenly, he began hearing the word mercy, mercy, and second chance, repeatedly.

Joel asked him how come he's able to see what went on inside the belly of the snake, because he supposed that someone swallowed by a snake will see nothing but pitch darkness.

Lee interjected and said there was this sudden flash of light that suddenly overshadowed the belly of that thing, that was when the bible in his pocket morphed into a man, he proceeded to say that he saw the man as he tried pulling him out of the belly of the monster. Lee became emotional and teary, and Joel urged him to stop taking, as he reminded him that his experience reflects what the saving grace of Christ can do.

"Guys, let's be fast about this before another drama erupts," said Kelvin.

"Professor, where are we going from here?" asked Chantell.

"We're going to Manicore and the day is far spent, we need to walk fast so darkness doesn't fall on us on our way," said Prof. Hendrix.

Immediately, after packing their things, they left the village of Humaita. Kimberly held Joel's hand as the students made their way out of the village of Humaita, and she suddenly developed this liking for her fiancée whom she seemed to have threatened to break off from. Joel's daring move to take Kimberley's place is an expression of love that suddenly blotted out every one of Joel's wrongs in Kimberley's bad book. She now sees Joel as a husband made from heaven for her, and unlike before, she now thinks Joel can be spontaneous when the need for spontaneity arises. More so, Lee's miraculous defeat of Ngala-na made Kimberley to be more appreciative of Joel's faith in God, because she knew that their victory over Ngala-na has everything to do with God's intervention. She now realised that her fiancé isn't just a guy blowing smoke about God, but someone with a fair knowledge of God's ability to do the impossible when men reach their limit.

Despite his too many troubles, Lee has unwittingly become the jewel in the crown as far as this research expedition is concerned. Lee and lucky and two words that never appears in a sentence because Lee was never lucky. This time his name isn't just associated with the word "lucky" because he escaped death by whiskers, his name is associated with the word "lucky" because Lee beat death with a bang.

After walking some distance, Lee looked overwhelmed as he turned back and waved good bye to this memorable village one last time, and funnily, Terry walked back and threw his hand around Lee's shoulder, then turned him around facing the road to Manicore.

They then joined the pack as they trekked to the town of Manicore. It was a very tiring journey because of the distance, and by the time they got to Manicore it was already dark and they arrived tired and weak. They went straight to the jungle lodge and paid for seven rooms in the lodge, which they shared among themselves as before. After asking the employees of the jungle lodge if they've seen his students but got a negative response, the professor tried dialling Collins and Mallon's phone number but the call didn't go through either. Professor Hendrix imbroglio is that every step he takes to rectify the situation gets out of hand and quickly morphs into something grimmer. Struggling with the whereabouts of his students, Professor Hendrix decided to put a phone call across to the university's vice chancellor. "Hello Professor," said Prof. Hendrix.

"Hello Professor, how're you and how's the research work going?" asked Prof. Tunsburry.

"We're fine for now, but how about the students I sent to pass a message across to you?" asked Prof. Hendrix.

"What students are you talking about, and what's the message about?" asked Prof. Tunsburry.

"We ran into some difficulties and I sent two of my students to inform the university authority that we might need some help," said Prof. Hendrix. The Vice Chancellor went blazing immediately he was told about the missing students. The news was corrosive to his ears and he didn't hesitate reading the riot act to Professor Hendrix, adding gasoline to the already incandescent and distressful situation. Professor Hendrix hinted the Vice Chancellor he supposed the students made contact with the university, but the already incensed Vice Chancellor said he doesn't have time for supposition as he urged Professor Hendrix to say what he's sure about.

"You're telling me two of your students are missing, or what?" asked Prof. Tunsburry. All effort to manage the situation seems to be falling apart, yet Professor Hendrix needs to find a way to wriggle himself out of this mess.

"Professor, I just want to know if they contacted the university authority". The Vice Chancellor doesn't seem ready to cut Professor Hendrix any slack, as he dug his heel further into the matter.

"What day did you send them on this errand, and when were they expected to call the school authority?" asked Prof. Tunsburry.

"That would be three days ago," said Prof. Hendrix.

"You mean they went missing three days ago and you're just searching for them now? And I don't think they contacted the university either, I should've been aware," said Prof. Tunsburry.

"Then let me search for them here, they may be putting up somewhere," said Prof. Hendrix. This isn't the kind of punchy conversation professor Hendrix wants to engage in at this moment, so he quickly ended the conversation with his Vice Chancellor to deal with the matter himself.

"First thing tomorrow morning, I'll call an emergency meeting, but I think you were negligent," said Prof. Tunsburry.

"With all due respect, Professor, I wasn't negligent in this, it's more complicated than you think," said Prof. Hendrix. Things have become thorny for the professor and extricating himself from this swamp might take more than necessary.

"Ok, search for them, and I'll call you tomorrow morning so we know the next step to take. Meanwhile, I'll make some calls about this tonight," the Vice Chancellor promised.

After the call to the university authority, Professor Hendrix informed his students of his findings. The whereabouts of Collins and Mallon is now the new puzzle that must be solved by the professor and his students. Funnily, Terry was the first person to get the hint that Collins and Mallon are now missing.

"Guys, Collins and Mallon didn't contact the university authority," said Terry.

"Then where did they go?" asked Kelvin.

"We've actually caused more trouble than we thought," said Vera.

"If only one could turn back the hands of the clock, we wouldn't have walked into that forest," said Kelvin.

"Guys, ask the workers in this lodge. Maybe they saw them by any chance," said Terry.

"They said they didn't come to the lodge," said Kelvin. The Professor walked in as his students discussed their debacle.

"Each one of you should take ten minutes rest, and then we'll all go around the town asking if they saw them by any chance," said Prof. Hendrix.

After having a brief rest the professor and his students went around the town of Manicore and continued to inquire of Collins and Mallon's whereabouts.

"Let's look for John Griffith, he might know their whereabouts. It's possible they're with him," said Amanda. Kelvin interjected and said that can be because John must have returned to Sao Paulo as discussed.

Interestingly, the conversation between Kelvin and Amanda got to the professor's ear. He turned around immediately and asked who John Griffith is, Kelvin interjected and said he's nobody.

Unfortunately, the professor was quite angry at Kelvin for his dismissive response, but Kelvin explained himself further saying he thinks it's not a line of inquiry worth pursuing as he doesn't intend to send the professor on a wild goose chase.

The professor immediately reminded Kelvin that it isn't within his gift to decide for him what line of inquiry to pursue or not, he then asked the students all they know about this John Griffith, funny enough the professor isn't willing to let this news lie fallow as he's determined to pursue any line of inquiry that could lead him to the whereabouts of Collins and Mallon.

Lee realised the professor expects them to be more open to avoid further casualty resulting from their exuberance and he then interjected immediately and told the professor all they knew about John Griffith. Interestingly, it isn't difficult fishing out the relatives of a British national in this remote part of the world.

As they went about the town of Manicore and asking if anyone sighted Collins and Mallon, they were at the same time asking about John Griffith. They eventually located the father in-law of John Griffith who told them John and Jain left for Sao Paulo days back and that Collins and Mallon didn't come looking for John at any time.

Sadly, they couldn't find any clue that showed Mallon and Collins got to Manicore, so the professor felt the best thing to do was to involve the police in that locality. Without hesitation they made their way to the local police station to officially inform them and seek their help.

"Hello, I'm Professor Hendrix at the University of Dartford in the United Kingdom," he said. "Ok professor, you're welcome, what can I do for you?" asked the Police officer.

The professor then told the police officer he sent his students for an important assignment in Manicore from the village of Humaita but they didn't return and he hasn't been able to find them. "What's the nature of the assignment?" asked the Police officer.

"They were to pass some information to the university authority in the United Kingdom," said Prof. Hendrix. The curious police officer was keen to know the nature of the assignment in question, particularly where the persons involved were foreigners. He made sure they are truly students on a research expedition as claimed, and then checked the identities of the professor and his students before opening a case of missing persons.

"Have you contacted the university they were meant to contact, to see if they heard from them?" asked the Police officer.

"Yeah, I did contact the school, but they said they didn't hear from them," said Prof. Hendrix. Police officers understand the exuberance and truancy of students, and this police officer needs to be sure that this is truly a case of missing students and not young men resting their heads in the bosoms of their newly found girlfriends.

"And you've not seen them since they left Humaita to Manicore?" asked the Police officer.

"No, I haven't.," replied Prof. Hendrix.

"Ok, we'll search the entirety of Manicore tonight. If we don't find them, then by tomorrow we'll search all the villages between Manicore and Humaita," said the Police officer. Professor Hendrix can't wait to get these students back to the United Kingdom, and the Vice Chancellor's stunning rebuke is a stark reminder of what's to come, and interestingly, the police will be the professor's last hope.

"Thank you, and please, I want you to do everything you can because these students are my responsibility," said Prof. Hendrix.

"Do you've their photographs?" asked the Police officer.

The professor turned to his students to see if they've Collins and Mallon's photographs. Unsurprisingly, the first thing the students did in the few minutes they spent resting in the jungle lodge was to charge their phones, and funnily, it's now coming handy in times such as this.

"Do any of you have Mallon and Collins' photographs anywhere?" asked Prof. Hendrix.

"Professor, I have Collins' photograph on my phone," said Lee.

"Professor, I have Mallon's photograph on my phone," said Johnny.

"Ok officer, you can have them," said Prof. Hendrix. He sent the photographs to the police officer's phone, and just as the professor and his students turned to leave the police station the police officer asked one last question.

"Where are you putting up, in case there's a need to reach you?" asked the Police officer.

"We're putting up at the jungle lodge; you can reach me with this phone number," said Prof. Hendrix.

Just as they turned to leave, the professor stopped and turned around facing the Police Officer as if he just remembered something to add to their conversation. Despite being told by John Griffith's father in-law that John and Jain have returned to Sao Paulo, the professor still brought up the idea that there's a possibility that his student met with John, and urged the Police Officer to explore that possibility further.

Interestingly, Professor Hendrix don't need to look any further as the Police Officer seem to know John personally, and said he saw John leave some days back to the airport as he returns to the city where he's based. He narrated to the professor that he was on patrol the other day with his men, when John was on his way to the airport with his wife in the car, John stopped to say hello to him and eventually continued after their brief conversation with him. He then assured the professor that he doesn't think his students established any contact with John who left days back with just his wife alone with him in the car. He however assured the professor that he has John's phone number and promised the professor that if their search fails to yield result, he might give John Griffith a phone call.

CHAPTER

SEVEN

Fifth Day in the Amazon

The next morning, the professor and his students' hurriedly rushed to the police station in anticipation for good news on the outcome of their search.

"Hello Professor, how was your night? I hope you slept well," asked the Police officer.

"Frankly speaking, officer, no one sleeps well in times such as this, and what's the outcome of your search last night?" asked Prof. Hendrix.

"We searched the entire town but there wasn't any trace of them, no one seems to have seen them," said the Police officer. The anxiety and despondency among the students increased and precipitated some inner unpleasantness towards Kelvin for setting off this rollercoaster of confusion in the first place. There was a thawing of relationships when Lee escaped Ngala-na but the news of Collins and Mallon seem to bring back those unpleasantnesses. It's obvious that when you're a hammer everything looks like a nail to you, the professor now considers everything suspicious, and even as the professor looks weak and tired like a man rescued from a drained pond, he's still willing to fight on until he finds Collins and Mallon.

"Officer, what do you suggest we do?" asked Prof. Hendrix.

"Let me assemble a search team, so we can help you search for them," said the Police officer.

"You're suggesting they may have been abducted or attacked on their way to this place?" asked Prof. Hendrix. The Police officer tried being quite pragmatic even as he remains reassuringly positive.

"Let's leave all possibilities open," said the Police officer.

About thirty minutes later, the police officer in charge of that station assembled a search team of four police officers to help with the search, accompanied by the professor and all his students with the exception of Collins and Mallon. Sadly, this isn't over until the fat lady sings, and just as they were about to leave, a phone call comes in from Professor Tunsburry, the university's Vice Chancellor.

"Good morning, how are you going with the search?" asked Prof. Tunsburry.

"We've informed the police, and they are assisting with the search," said Prof. Hendrix.

"You mean you're just informing the police about the missing students? Today makes it the fourth day!" exclaimed Prof. Tunsburry.

"I had to secure the other students first, but it's more complicated than you think," said Prof. Hendrix.

This research expedition has been a crashing failure in all spheres and Professor Hendrix's pain can't be moralised, but it now behoves on the professor to stem these failures going forward.

"This is a case of gross negligence on your part. You have to do everything to make sure those students are found safe, and sound," Prof. Tunsburry retorted.

"I'm already doing everything I can to find them, and I promise you I'll bring them back to the United Kingdom safe and sound," Prof. Hendrix assured.

Even though the odds are quite visibly stacked against him, Professor Hendrix remained optimistic, that he'll get his student's back to the United Kingdom in one piece. After all, providence was on his side when he was faced with Ngala-na, and this time the mountain is less steep.

"I'm informing the Foreign Office about this right away," said Prof. Tunsburry.

"Professor, I don't think it's a good idea," Prof. Hendrix retorted.

"This institution can't afford to make the headlines for the wrong reasons," said Prof. Tunsburry.

Professor Hendrix understands that there isn't any need getting his feathers in the flutter, and the absurdity of his story will continue to astound his Vice Chancellor. It's now glaringly obvious that his boss has refused to be a puppet on the strings this time as he decided to put his foot down, and will never consent to being led the garden path by Professor Hendrix and still be all smiles about it.

"We're at it, and I'll get back to you as soon as something comes up," said Prof. Hendrix. This isn't just a blast from the past, this adventure is dishing up its worst to this professor in quite a calm but cruel way. Sadly, the surprises are in composite and the fact that his troubles comes in piece meal as he grapples to contain the unfolding drama, makes his effort to contain the situation anything but a mockery.

The police search team, together with the professor and his students moved from village to village in their search for Mallon and

Collins. Firstly, they arrived at the village of Karante but there isn't any positive result.

"We've gone round this village, and we've asked questions as well. None of them saw your students," said the Police officer.

"Maybe we should ask more people. Someone must know something about them," said Prof. Hendrix.

"Officer, let's search the bushes around, before moving forward," Johnny proposed.

"Are you suggesting they may've been attacked by wild animals?" asked the Police officer. The students think it necessary to put Johnny's comment into proper perspective to help the search.

"It may not necessarily be wild animals, they may've been attacked by some rascals in this village, you never can tell," said Tyler. "Let's get some villagers to assist us with searching the bushes," the Police officer proposed as he takes Tyler's suggestion on board. The professor understands that money motivates, and he's willing to part with his cash just to get the desired result.

"Tell them, I don't mind paying them for their services provided they help me locate them; at least they know this forest more," said Prof. Hendrix.

"They were riding bicycles; if they find their bicycles, then we might use the bicycles to trace them," said Prof. Hendrix. They searched all of the bushes around the village of Karante, but there wasn't any trace of Collins and Mallon.

While in the village of Parana, its breakfast time and Kamti brought fruits to Collins and Mallon, since they've both refused to eat the villagers' food.

"My friends, how're you?" Kamti asked as he walked in. "I told you not to call us that," said Mallon.

"Awe! Why, my friends, why?" exclaimed Kamti.

"If you were our friend you would've helped us make contact with our people to let them know we are locked up here," said Mallon. Mallon continued with his flurry of tantrums while pacing up and down, Collins decided to apply nicety to help win Kamti to their side.

"We'll give you plenty of money, money to change your life, and I equally have a lot of nice things. I'll give them to you," Collins promised.

"You know my king will punish me for that," said Kamti.

"We aren't asking you to help us escape, if you let our people know where we're, no one will know about it," said Collins. Sadly, all the money in the world isn't enough to make Kamti switch sides because loyalty to his people comes before money.

"I brought you those fruits you used to like," said Kamti.

"I'm tired of eating fruit; I just want to leave this cell," Collins retorted.

"Can't you see we've grown very lean? Why can't you just help us?" cried Mallon.

"I can't, my friends. I'll get you more fresh fruit later today," said Kamti. After succeeding to steer the conversation from helping the prisoners escape to getting them fresher fruits, the emotional Kamti left Collins and Mallon in the cell but with a heavy heart did he leave them.

"This is our fourth day of incarceration, where's the professor?" cried Mallon.

"I don't know, Mallon. Maybe he's somewhere looking for us, and I just don't know what to say," Collins said as he sheds tears. Mallon became petty again as his emotion got the best of him, he's disappointed in Kamti whose hands are tied, the village head who kept him in prison and even his professor who should've come to their rescue but failed to do so.

"I told you the professor is a disappointment," said Mallon.

"Let's not say that, Mallon. Let's just hope for a miracle of some sort," said Collins who remained hopeful.

"How do we hope for a miracle, if the professor that's supposed to get us out is busy with his science research?" asked Mallon, who remained unconvinced that someone out there is searching for them.

"I don't know what else to do, but we need to be positive to survive this, and I'm equally confused," said Collins.

Three and a half hours after they finished with the village of Karante, the police and the search team moved to the village of Ginrtete, yet there wasn't any trace of Collins and Mallon. The search team then proceeded to the next village, and the next, until they arrived at the village of Parana where Collins and Mallon are being held.

Although the case of the missing students had been reported to the Foreign Office by the university authority an hour earlier and the Foreign Office has just issued a public statement, resulting in the story of the missing students making the headlines in the United Kingdom.

The police officer spoke with some natives of Parana who confirmed that two white boys were arrested some days earlier.

"Professor, they said two white males on bicycles were arrested here a few days ago," said the Police officer.

"Find out where they were taken to," said Prof. Hendrix. The police officer made further enquiries about the whereabouts of the arrested students.

"They said they were in the custody of the village head," said the Police officer.

"That's wrong, why would he do a thing like that? I know the village head, and he seems to be a reasonable man," said Prof. Hendrix in an outburst of anger.

"Professor, have you been here before?" asked Terry.

"Yes, but that was five years ago, and this was the village we conducted our research," the professor confirmed. All the students looked at the professor in surprise, except Joel whom the professor told about his previous expedition while in a conversation on a plane.

"But there was nothing like Ngala-na the python?" asked Kelvin.

"Of course not, we worked with the instructions of the people," said Prof. Hendrix.

"The professor is right, if we had not gone into that forest on our own we wouldn't have spent the night with Ngala-na," said Terry.

"And we wouldn't have been looking for Collins and Mallon," said Prof. Hendrix. Minutes later, the search party arrived at the village head's palace, and after exchanging pleasantries, the police officer went straight into the business of the day.

"We've come for the two white males you arrested," said the Police officer.

"I arrested them because they were wandering around my village," said the village head. Just as he opened his mouth to respond to the police officer, there was a flicker of recognition as the village head immediately recognised Professor Hendrix as one of those that stole his bronze head.

"You're one of them," said the village head. The amazed professor shockingly asked, "what's he saying, and why's he pointing at me?"

"He said you're one of them," said the Police officer. "Ok, yes, I was one of those that came here five years ago, but I want to see my students," said Prof. Hendrix. The police officer turned to the village head.

"Please bring me the boys in your custody," said the Police officer. The village head sent for Collins and Mallon to be brought out, and yet he continues to point his finger of accusation at the professor.

"It's because of you, these boys suffered," said the village head. Rattled by the finger pointing, the professor queried the village head's boisterousness.

"Why is he pointing at me?" asked Prof. Hendrix.

"He said it's because of you these boys suffered," said the Police officer.

Life sometimes can be funny, we carry a little baggage around and no one knows about it until a mess from the past resurfaces somehow.

"We never had any problems the last time we were here, so how does this relate to me?" asked Prof. Hendrix.

Not long afterwards, Collins and Mallon came out and saw the professor, the police officers, and all the other students including the missing seven. Collins was filled with joy and turned to Mallon.

"Mallon, I told you to believe in miracles," said Collins. Mallon went into contrition and self-confession.

"Professor, I thought you forgot about us and continued with your research, I'm sorry for not having enough faith in you," said Mallon.

Seeing how emaciated the boys were, the professor shed tears, though was relived to find the boys alive.

"What did they do to deserve this?" cried Prof. Hendrix. Seeing the emotional trauma of the professor and his student, the police officer turned to the village head.

"You know your action is against the law," said the Police officer.

"But I told you, they were wandering in my village," the village head retorted.

"Then you should've called the police, not lock them up," said the Police officer.

The village head pointed at the professor as he tried to justify his actions.

"When they came here five years ago, ask him, I welcomed them but they betrayed my hospitality by stealing the bronze head of our masquerade," said the village head. The police officer inquired further in his bid to explore this village head's accusation, he then turned to the professor.

"He said five years ago, one of you, or all of you stole the bronze head of their masquerade," said the Police officer.

"That was all he kept saying, as the reason he locked us up," said Collins. Eyes are now on the professor who must set the record straight.

"Tell him none of us did such a thing. My colleague bought the bronze head from a native of this village, and we never knew he stole it, he told us it was his," said Prof. Hendrix.

"Are you sure of this?" asked the village head.

"Of course, yes. I know the house of the man that sold it to us," said Prof. Hendrix.

"It's good you're here, because I've been blaming your people for this. Take me to the house of that person," said the village head. The professor agreed, and it didn't take long before they set off in this fact finding mission. They walked some distance along the meandering foot path in the village, and interestingly, the professor's memory didn't fail him in this critical moment. Suddenly, there was a flicker of recognition, and the professor pointed at Teiaka, who just returned from the farm and was standing in the front of his hut.

"He sold it to us, I remember his face vividly," said Prof. Hendrix.

"Teiaka, is it true? And you allowed me to punish these innocent boys," yelled the village head.

"My lord, I didn't do anything," Teiaka protested.

"If I bring the chief priest here, will you say you didn't?" the stern looking village head asked.

"My lord, please don't bring the chief priest. I did it, I stole it and sold it to them, and I told them it was mine," said Teiaka. The police officer decided to interpret the unfolding drama and what was being said to the professor and his students.

"Professor, he accepted he stole it, and also accepted he told your friend it was his own," said the Police officer.

"And he locked us up like thieves for days?" said Mallon, as he screamed at the village head. The village head became unwittingly remorseful over his heavy handedness and misjudgement, and then turned to the professor.

"I am sorry, I just found out the truth, because I've blamed you people for years," said the village head. He also turned to Collins and Mallon and apologised unreservedly.

"My friends, I'm very, very sorry about everything. Teiaka will later be punished for this," said the village head.

This village head didn't take likely the fact that he has inadvertently been accusing the wrong people for the theft of his bronze head, and when these guests leave, Teiaka will have a lot to answer for.

The police officer watched as apologies were said and accepted, and now that the boys are found and the pack is now complete, it's time to return home in one piece.

"We've to get going, it's now over, and there's nothing we can do about that," said Prof. Hendrix. Not yet, because apologies that were said and accepted by the parties involved isn't enough to right these wrongs, and Vera has bones to pick because some injustices haven't been addressed. Vera then turned to the police officer as she wants to see to it that this village head is punished.

"Aren't you going to arrest him? "she asked.

"This has been settled amicably, so let's let the sleeping dog lie," said the Police officer.

"But he broke the law, and that was unlawful detention," Vera insists.

"Ok, should I arrest him, and arrest your professor as well for buying stolen goods? I said, let the sleeping dog lie," the Police officer chuckled. Realising that addressing this injustice isn't just as simple as black and white, Vera had to accept the suggestion of the police officer to let the sleeping dog lie.

The professor, his students, and the team of police officers then left the village of Parana and made their way to Manicore. This adventure was nothing short of a toxic cocktail of greed, barbarism and betrayal and will scarcely be missed as these students turned their back to this research project in the Amazon forest for good.

After an interesting reunion and catching up as they made their way to Manicore, they eventually arrived the Jungle lodge. The professor felt excitingly relieved that no one would be holding a gun to his head and asking him to explain the whereabouts of his students.

It's now time to unwind after drawing the curtain on this drama.

"Officer, I'm inviting you and your team to join us for drinks at the lodge later," said Prof. Hendrix.

"Is it necessary?" asked the Police officer.

"We just want to show our appreciation for what you did for us," said Prof. Hendrix.

"We're just doing our job, Professor," said the Police officer.

"Ok, but I insist, see it as a friend inviting you for drink," said Prof. Hendrix.

"Ok, we'll be there by 7pm," the police officer promised.

"Thank you," said Prof. Hendrix. Even as the professor expressed his gratitude, Collins and Mallon remained forever grateful to the team of police officers who came to their rescue.

"Officer, thank you for your help, you've saved me a great deal of torture," said Collins. The Police officer bursts into laughter.

"I'm glad you're fine now," said the Police officer. They shook hands and returned to their jungle lodge while the police officers returned to their duty. Mallon seems not to have had enough of the heart aches.

"Professor, what about the research we came for?" asked Mallon.

"The research is now consigned to the future. We all need to go back home," said Prof. Hendrix.

The moment the professor and his students arrived at the town of Manicore, his phone rang, and it was his wife, Anne.

"Hello honey, how are you?" asked Prof. Hendrix.

"I'm fine; and I've been trying to reach you on the phone for the past two hours," said Anne.

"Are you ok? You know there isn't network in the village we're supposed to be doing our research work," said Prof. Hendrix.

"What's this story of missing students that's over all the headlines?" asked Anne.

"Oh no, Why can't this nightmare just go away!" exclaimed Prof. Hendrix. The professor's troubles just metamorphosed from a jungle drama into a national one. The cloud seems to have moved from one place and gathered somewhere else without dispersing. Arguably, the professor's experience in the jungle was nothing but calm before the storm.

"Are you ok?" asked Anne.

"I suppose so, I told Professor Tunsburry to hold on but he didn't listen.

"Is it true, are the students missing?" asked Anne.

"Yes, but I've found them," said Prof. Hendrix.

"Ok, that's good. At least this will help to end any panic the news has created," said Anne.

This isn't some sort of trumped up witch hunt from the Vice Chancellor, he's just being careful, aside the fact that he isn't willing to stick his neck out on the butchers table to be chopped off in the most casual and cruel way.

The university campus is now awash with journalists, with some tailing the Vice Chancellor around for answers to questions in the minds of friends and relatives of these students. He isn't skirting the questions begging for answers, he's obviously trying to manage the situation because he isn't ready to be burnt on the stake either.

Now that things continued to go south even as the professor tries to hold them together, the only way to turf this matter will be to apply his damage control skills.

"I'll call Professor Tunsburry to let him know I've found the students, so he can issue a statement immediately," said Prof. Hendrix.

"What actually happened?" asked Anne. The professor is in no mood to tell his sad tale, and he has now chosen to marshal his energy wisely to avoid turning things up a notch.

"Anne, it's a long story, and I can't talk about it now. Let me call the professor right away," said Prof. Hendrix. Professor Hendrix called Professor Tunsburry immediately to update him on the latest developments.

"Hello Professor, have you found the students?" asked Prof. Tunsburry.

"Yes, I've found them," he replied, and expressed a sigh of relief.

"Thank goodness, I'll have to issue a press statement to stop any panic from the students' parents," said Prof. Tunsburry.

Professor Hendrix seemed a little peeved with his boss, because he considers the Vice Chancellor's vicarious atonement to be quite hasty and unnecessary, but all he could do is to mutter his frustration.

"But I suggested you give me a little time before involving the Foreign Office," Prof. Hendrix retorted.

"What if you hadn't found them? The government would've blamed the university for not seeking the assistance of the Foreign Office," said Prof. Tunsburry. The Vice Chancellor isn't willing to throw caution to the wind and he's the kind of man who believes that being a kid doesn't mean you can't hit the child with a glove, but at least you can use a kid's glove. In similar vein, the Vice Chancellor isn't going to spare his favourite professor if he falters, and Professor Hendrix seem to get the drill. It's now arguably obvious that the Vice Chancellor will never acquiesce keeping this under wraps, particularly when his students' safety is at stake, which consequently meant his own job as the Vice Chancellor of this university is also on the line.

"Oh, you're considering the political impact on the school, while I'm considering the psychological impact on the parents," said Prof. Hendrix.

"Are you continuing your research or you're coming back?" asked Prof. Tunsburry.

"We're coming back, let's all return home safely," said Prof. Hendrix.

"Ok, I'll arrange for a chartered flight to bring you back immediately," said Prof. Tunsburry.

Armed with the understanding that adults don't point a loaded gun at the heart of what they do. The Vice Chancellor quickly ended the phone conversation and rushed to attend to the press that's already waiting to hear from him. That night at the jungle lodge, the police officers, the professor, and the students, spent some quality time as they merry until about 10pm. Yet, later that night, the professor remembered to call Professor Santos.

"Hello Professor, how's your research work going?" asked Prof. Santos.

"It didn't go well, so we're going back to the United Kingdom," said Prof. Hendrix.

"What happened? Didn't you get the plant species you were interested in?" asked Prof. Santos.

The awfulness of this expedition left Professor Hendrix speechless for a while, sadly he can't remain speechless for too long over his fear of reliving his Amazonian experience over again.

"We did, but my students entered into their forest without a guide and from there, one thing led to the other and we'd to end the expedition abruptly," said Prof. Hendrix.

Sadly, the professor's sanguine presupposition concerning this trip wasn't one that was realisable with the two many twists and turns from the get go.

"That's what happens when dealing with young people. Are your students ok?" asked Prof. Santos.

"Yes, they're ok, and we'll talk about the details later," said Prof. Hendrix.

Professor Santos smiled and said it's a shame it ended this way, he then likened Professor Hendrix's research expedition to a rabbit being dead even before it's pulled out of the hat.

"Hmm, I'm miffed by this whole saga, but it seems the rabbit in your story died of the heat inside the hat," said Prof. Hendrix.

"Ok, when is your flight, and when are you leaving Manicore?" asked Prof. Santos.

"The university is making arrangements for a chartered flight for us for tomorrow," said Prof. Hendrix.

The two professors had hoped to spend time discussing the outcome of this research expedition.

"Then there isn't any need for me to come down to Manicore to see you," said Prof. Santos.

"No, there isn't a need for that, but I'll call you when we touch down in London," said Prof. Hendrix.

The Vice Chancellor was true to his word, as he arranged a chattered flight to bring the professor and his student home immediately. The next morning the professor addressed his students as they were about to board their plane.

"I want you all to know that the press will be waiting to use your sad experiences to sell their papers," said Prof. Hendrix. This whole saga has been made more awful because both the professor and his students have been scarred by this experience, and sadly, the situation tends to remain volatile as the involvement of the press could mean things flying off the handle.

"Professor, what do we do about it?" asked Beata.

"You should keep your story to yourselves until after the school authority have finished their inquiry," said Prof. Hendrix.

"What sort of inquiry are you talking about?" asked Vera.

"A disciplinary panel to look into this trip, so I'll advise you all to finish with the university before you open your mouth to the press," said Prof. Hendrix.

"Does the university have to do that? They should be happy we're safe," said Mallon.

It's common knowledge that Mallon is a self-pitying young man whose naivety cuts across living in denial of the reality before him and throwing petty tantrums when the rubber hits the road, but Collins is just the opposite.

"Mallon, things aren't done that way. Your story has already made headlines," said Prof. Hendrix.

"Who will face the disciplinary panel then?" asked Beata.

"Everyone and that includes me. No more questions go and board your plane," said Prof. Hendrix.

Later in the evening the students and the professor arrive in the United Kingdom and the press was all over them like wet clothes, wanting to hear and report on their story. Weaving through the crowd of journalists seamlessly and staying mum, they all kept their experiences to themselves as instructed. As the students focused on leaving the airport without giving out anything to the press, Kelvin stood looking frustrated as he beckoned on Amanda who seemed to be dawdling to hasten up, but she seem to be troubled because she couldn't find her mobile phone.

Kelvin had to stay back to assist in the search but after trying laboriously, they still didn't find her phone.

By morning of the next day, Professor Hendrix was with the Vice Chancellor. "Good to see you, Professor. How was your flight yesterday?" asked Prof. Tunsburry.

"Our flight was fine, at least we landed safely," said Prof. Hendrix.

"Did your students grant audience to the press?" asked Prof. Tunsburry.

"No, because I told them not to," said Prof. Hendrix.

The Vice Chancellor is a regular professor who doesn't just tick boxes but does things by the book. This might mean holding the feet of his favourite professor to the fire if need be because he isn't bothered by people thinking the worst of him.

The disciplinary panel will commence the day after tomorrow, and I'll be in that panel. That's when I'll want to hear your story," said Prof. Tunsburry.

"I think if you hear my story now, there wouldn't be a need for the panel you're talking about," said Prof. Hendrix.

"This institution must do what it thinks is right, and this panel is the right way to go about it," said Prof. Tunsburry.

Two days later, the disciplinary panel instigated by the university commenced their hearing and Professor Hendrix is the first to take the stand.

"Professor Hendrix, thank you for coming. Please tell this panel everything you know that resulted in two of your students getting lost," said the Vice Chancellor.

"Ok, thank you for giving me the opportunity to clear the confusion. The first day we arrived in the village of Humaita, which is supposed to be where we were meant to carry out our research. I told the students to rest until the next day when a guide would lead us through the forest. Minutes later, they said they wanted to have a walk within the village but ended up walking seven kilometres into the forest, so I decided to enter the forest with the rest of the students to search for them with the help of the natives, and sadly there wasn't any help available from the natives. The next day I had to send Collins Lancaster and Mallon Vincent to go to the town of Manicore to make contact with the university authority, while I lead the search for the student in the forest. Unfortunately, Collins and Mallon were abducted halfway, and finally I had to do everything I could to recover both the missing students and the abducted students.

"Some of the students interviewed talked about their encounter with a giant snake, what'll you tell us about that?" asked Prof. Logan.

The missing seven, as I called them, told me of how they stole the diamond belonging to a fourteen-meter long python. The python got angry and came destroying everything in the village, and the chief priest decided to offer one of the students as a sacrifice to the snake. Luckily, he survived and we left the village immediately.

Professor Logan laughed, making mockery of his fellow professors' tale. "Is there anything like a fourteen-meter long snake?" asked Prof. Logan.

"I'm a professor like you and I deal with facts, not fiction. I saw the snake myself when she later came to the village venting her anger," said Prof. Hendrix. Professor Hendrix isn't a sensationalist and neither is he a fatalist who's keen on pulling one of his per-fidious manoeuvres, and selling conspiracy isn't is strength either because he's just a man who tells it as it is.

"Don't you think it's negligent of you taking the students to such a dangerous place?" asked Prof. Greg.

"If we'd worked with the guide, no student would've been lost, and there wouldn't be an encounter with the snake in the middle of the night inside the forest. For your information, walking as far as seven kilometres into the forest, even here in Britain, will result in an encounter with something wild," said Prof. Hendrix.

The next day, Lee Farrell appeared before the disciplinary panel.

"Lee Farrell, you're welcomed to this panel. Please tell us why you decided to go after the snake's diamond in a manner that put your course mates in danger?" asked Prof. Tunsburry.

"Professor, my course mates were over a hundred meters away from where the diamond was, and after succeeding to get the diamond, I ran in the opposite direction, so I wouldn't lead the snake to them," said Lee.

"How come you travelled with such military grade equipments to your place of research?" asked Prof. Logan.

"My dad told me there are jaguars in those forests, so I decided to take some of his military equipment for self-defence," said Lee.

"How come you were chosen for the sacrifice?" asked Prof. Greg.

"A lot was cast and it fell on Kimberly, but I decided to give myself up for her, since I was the one who got their god angry," said Lee.

After Lee finished with the panel, he turned to leave but Professor Logan suddenly came up with one last question.

"I find your assertion that your bible turned into a man to rescue you from the belly of the snake laughable, don't you?" asked Prof. Logan.

"With all due respect, Professor, you didn't go into the belly of the beast with me, I know what I saw. That thing isn't just a snake, it's a spirit, and the bible in my pocket reigned supreme and saved me from that demonic snake," said Lee.

A day later, Terry Morgan appeared before the disciplinary panel.

"Terry Morgan, you're welcomed to this panel. Please tell us why you joined Lee in stealing the diamond from the snake," asked Prof. Tunsburry.

"I joined Lee because I realised if I didn't help him he may not make it out alive," said Terry.

"But you encouraged Lee to do this in the first place?" asked Prof. Logan.

"I only asked him about his strategy as per getting the diamond, and realised he would make it if well executed, so I encouraged him," said Terry.

Two weeks later, the university authority published the decision of the panel after the students and their professor spent two days narrating their tales of cowardice and brigandage to the university's disciplinary panel.

The university authority apologised to Professor Hendrix for the troubles his students put him through, and also thanked him for making effort to find the missing students and securing the release of the abducted students. He was discharged of any wrongdoing, and as a way of compensation, the university promised to fund his future research work.

Lee Farrell and Terry Morgan were given warning letters by the university authority for engaging in acts that put their course mates in danger.

Finally, the rest of the students were discharged of any wrongdoing.

Immediately the university disciplinary panel finished sitting, Lee became a known campus evangelist preaching, 'Jesus saves,' in the university campus. His central message is his testimony about his encounter with Ngala-na, and how Jesus came to his rescue. He is now a pastor of a church in London.

On their arrival at Heathrow airport weeks back, Amanda serendipitously lost her phone. Unfortunately, within days of losing her phone, a nude video Amanda made of herself and Kevin frolicking with each other in the motel room they rented separately for themselves in the jungle lodge in Manicore found its way from her phone to the internet. The leak brought Amanda a great emotional distress as she became an object of mockery among her mates within and outside the university campus. The shame took a toll on her as she couldn't cope with her studies in the university, and despite the considerable time spent in counselling, she had to quit her university education. Kelvin on the other hand was troubled by the leak but continued his study and finished his university education successfully.

Joel and Kimberly walked down the aisle and said, yes, I do, to each other. They got married not long after their university education. Joel now pastors' a mega church in America, enjoying the support of his wife, Kimberly, who became a devoted Christian in the wake of Lee's defeat of Ngala-na.

Days after the university authority exonerated Professor Hendrix of any wrong doing, he visited Lee just after sunset. They then walked and sat in a quiet part of the park and continued their conversation as though they are mates. The professor took his time to hear Lee's story as he's keen to know what transpired in the belly of Ngala-na and how it came about that the monster spewed him out. Lee narrated exactly the story he told Joel, how he heard the echoes of mercy reverberates in the belly of the beast and the sudden bright light that flooded the belly of Ngala-na, before the bible in his pocket turned into the man that rescued him.

"And you're convinced that the man is Jesus?" asked the professor.

"Who else will be it, if not Jesus?" replied Lee.

"I will like to meet this your Jesus, because He worth's knowing," said Prof. Hendrix.

By Sunday morning, Professor Hendrix was the first in church, and was also the first to attend to the alter call. This marks the beginning of the professor's Christian faith.

Books by Boniface Ossai

www.ingramcontent.com/pod-product-compliance
Lightning Source LLC
Chambersburg PA
CBHW070950180726
48291CB00004B/1223

9 781913 438654